To Pastor

Hope you enjoy this — It's given with love and thanks for all you do to serve others in His name —

In Christ,

David Bellin

The Marble King

and Other Stories

The Marble King

and Other Stories

David Bellin

Epigraph Books
Rhinebeck, NY

The Marble King and Other Stories copyright 2014 by David Bellin

All rights reserved. No part of this book may be used or reproduced in any manner without written permission from the author except in critical articles or reviews.

Contact the publisher for information.

Printed in the United States of America

Book and cover design by Chris Hallman

Library of Congress Control Number: 2015930390

Hardcover ISBN: 978-1-936940-99-8

Paperback ISBN: 978-1-936940-98-1

Epigraph Books
22 East Market Street, Suite 304
Rhinebeck, NY 12572
www.epigraphps.com

FOR MAX.
Never a false note.

This is a work of fiction. Names, characters, locations, institutions and incidents are either the author's invention or are used fictitiously. Any resemblance to actual persons living or dead is unintentional.

The stories, *Endings* and *Friday, Daddy*, contain sexual references. The passages are neither explicit nor overt. Nevertheless, they may be beyond the boundaries set for young people in individual families and parental discretion is advised.

CONTENTS

The Wingback Chair 1

Dialogue in D flat 15

Witnesses 25

Brownstone 1940 37

Endings 55

Adoption 63

Meter Maid 83

The Vienna Game 99

Front Matter 125

Friday, Daddy 133

Brownstone 1942 151

The Marble King 171

Forgive him.

A new husband, even the most caring,
will misread moods
with breathtaking blindness…

The Wingback Chair

You might be surprised to learn that in a marriage between two people who love each other deeply one of them, the wife in this case, is quite capable of concealing a private resentment from the other.

Or perhaps you wouldn't be surprised.

That implies a bit of experience on your part so I'll proceed, confident you'll see why a tall, graceful and much pursued young lady, Melissa Beale by name, would give herself joyfully to a shorter, somewhat rotund man twelve years her senior, Malcolm Witherspoon, who resembled a pigeon.

Well, you say, there must have been a bit of hawk in him also, to attract a desirable woman.

You *are* experienced.

And hawk there was in Malcolm, made known in those moments when the gentle fluttering vanished, his head jutted forward, his eyes narrowed and it was clear this man would have his way in those matters he truly cared about.

The Marble King and Other Stories

She saw it first when he told her father that Andrew Jackson was wrong in eliminating the Second Bank, that the loss of unified currency would encourage speculators and erode the nation's economy. He followed with specific examples of nearby merchants whose profits for the ensuing year, 1834, would be threatened by the inability to set future rates.

Melissa was little impressed by such faraway concepts as future rates but acutely impressed by the five seconds of silence after Malcolm's words. Never in her memory had her father been speechless that long in any debate, and the opponent was not even one of his moneyed friends, someone whose opinion had a measure of wealth to support it, but a young priest, newly ordained in their Episcopal parish and invited as a routine courtesy to tea.

It was a delicious interval. She was sitting quietly in the drawing room with her mother, the men just outside at the threshold of the veranda, silhouettes visible through gauzy drapes, and a glance flashed between the two women that said, "Oh?"

In the older woman it bespoke gleeful satisfaction but there's little purpose in pursuing that here. More to our point, in the younger woman it bespoke a stirring within, followed by a faint reddening of fair cheeks without, and the emergence of the most implausible idea. I mean, really, Melissa, she murmured into her fan, he comes up to your eyebrows, what will that look like at the wedding?

It looked just fine, of course. By then, Malcolm was measured by his stature in the pulpit and that was commanding, indeed. Did I mention our setting was Savannah, that sheltered seaport where endless bales of cotton departed and endless bales of money arrived? Blessed by such bounty, the parish church, St. Thomas, had grown into one of those monumental Anglican structures of endless stained glass, vaulted ceiling, polished mahogany pews, two-tiered choir gallery and a chancel that seemed both a mile away and treetop high, a place where even a tall priest might be dwarfed. But not Malcolm.

Facing his congregation, he occupied the space as Gabriel himself might, delivering sermons of uncommon clarity in a voice that filled even the distant narthex. More, unlike his predecessors who dithered when faced with congregational squabbles over committee appointments or choir selections, Malcolm handled such matters instantly, with sensible solutions reinforced, if necessary, by a formidable glint of the eye.

And so at the wedding, the attending priest might well have been saying "I now pronounce you cathedral and wife" for all that the actual difference in height mattered. In truth, of course, Melissa did wed the edifice that was St. Thomas by marrying its master.

She was content with that, especially since a church must include a vicarage to house the priest and his family. The parish being as prosperous as it was, the St. Thomas vicarage was none of your cottage-like afterthoughts to the main building but a brick manse of a dozen rooms, all sun-filled and spacious, all opening on a veranda or balcony, and all gleaming with parquet floors and mirrors and pottery and love seats and veneered desks and lacquered cabinetry on a scale to make Queen Anne herself feel at home.

It certainly made Melissa feel that way. She wandered about in the sweet embrace of the familiar, planning to switch the placement of a desk and a china display and possibly put brighter drapery sashes in a few rooms, the sort her mother always knew where to find—nothing radical, just tiny touches here and there, and perhaps she could arrange a more prominent location for one particular chair, a delicate little wingback, so much like the one in her family front parlor, a childhood favorite, the same rose fabric, the same subtle inward slant to the sides to preserve body warmth (my chair wants to hug me!), the same stubby cabriole legs, the same silly padded feet —

"It's way past time to sweep all this out and bring in simple pine and cherrywood furnishings, isn't it?" asked Malcolm.

Forgive him.

New husbands, even the most caring, will misread moods with breathtaking blindness.

From the replies swirling through Melissa's mind, she selected the one that seemed shrewdest.

"Of course, dear, and we would do it if the church weren't so grand, but we can't have visitors stepping from a palace into, well, a farmhouse."

"Aha!" answered Malcolm. "Why not?"

A sermon followed, delivered to a congregation of one by a preacher with head thrust forward and voice firm, radiating conviction that a church must present a majestic front to properly frame the word of God and celebrate His glory, while a priest, who is only God's instrument, must present himself simply and humbly. Consider the example of their own Episcopal church, he exhorted, with its blend of Latinate opulence and Lutheran modesty.

He smiled in artless triumph at the power of this illustration and Melissa smiled back, but not at her husband's learned example, which she heard but dimly. She smiled instead at the involuntary way the preacher held the congregation's hand as he orated, bestowing feathery caresses first to palm, then to shoulder, then to chin, then to cheek, then back to hand, where the circuit would begin anew.

She regarded the remarkable scene: Malcolm's forceful side, so publicly applauded, and Malcolm's tender side, a new bride's secret treasure, both on display at once and both directed at her and her alone.

The hollow place inside her began to fill. Furniture, she told herself, just furniture. She might honestly enjoy selecting new pine and cherrywood items. Just furniture, except—she tried to resist the thought—except for the little chair with the padded feet.

"Which item should we keep for comparison between old and new?" she asked casually.

"Why, none of them, my love. It would look as if we were inviting judgment of the former priests."

"Of course, dear."

"Merely exploring my home, a natural thing to do," she explained to an imaginary questioner as she wandered the cavernous attic. Not needed for living space with all the rooms below, the area had become a repository for assorted mysterious shapes beneath faded muslin sheets. Cautiously lifting the musty cloths, she uncovered dented steamer trunks, a pair of doorless armoires, a cracked lectern, a six-foot long mural of the Savannah river, a jib from some small sailing craft, a spinning wheel missing its pedal, several rusty lampstands, a Revolutionary War musket rack and—cheerful discovery—boxes of wooden toys, ready for play. Just a little dusting...

That could wait, of course. More important right now was a location she spotted beneath one of the attic's narrow dormered windows, a place where light filtered down, enough light for sewing or crocheting or the moments of meditation and personal prayer a priest's wife should be granted.

Malcolm left her in complete charge of the refurnishing, so it was easy enough to spirit the little chair upstairs during the

The Marble King and Other Stories

moving days, especially since the workers were slaves borrowed from Melissa's family, long-time house servants who no doubt saw the resemblance to her prized wingback at home. When she said nothing about it, neither did they and the chair went to the attic in conspiratorial silence.

Melissa, a social animal from the cradle, now began to find occasional solitude a companion. As a pastor's wife, of course, she was the organizer of teas, women's meetings, charity projects, dinners—not to mention her continuing role as the belle of the showy parties her own family favored—and she handled it all with cheery and genuine excitement, an excitement spiced by the universal esteem for her husband. She spent as much time as she could at Malcolm's side during these affairs, basking with innocent pleasure in the attention they drew.

At the same time, there were those tiptoe climbs to the attic now and again when Malcolm was occupied at church, a retreat for Melissa into the dulcet light of the dormered window and the gentle arms of her little wingback, crochet pattern and a book of psalms in hand, for an hour or so of reflection—*connecting* is the way she saw it, linking herself to Malcom, to St. Thomas, to God, to the future—finding a unity that left her peacefully fulfilled.

The birth of Malcolm Junior halted the retreats. The dusty toys came down from the attic, a comforting reminder to Melissa of what lay overhead but no trips were made during the child's early years, the lure of the attic far outweighed by the delight of nurturing, and at times simply watching, her exceptional little boy. His physique, long and supple, was definitely his mother's and his mental grasp, astonishingly quick and precocious, just as definitely from his father. One day at naptime, when the house was quiet and she had put her son in his crib, she found herself actually waltzing across the room with joy at this rosy-cheeked validation of her union with Malcolm.

6

The boy turned out to be their only child, a condition that brought some wistful longing to the couple now and again, but those moments vanished quickly. The doctor had found an irregular heartbeat in Melissa while she was carrying little Malcolm, giving some concern about further deliveries and, to be candid, little Malcolm was so bright, so handsome and so loving that he filled the days; it was hard to imagine sharing time with any siblings.

Formal education started with his sixth year. Tutors took over the mornings and then most afternoons as well, and Melissa re-discovered the attic, slipping up the stairs two or three times a week for an hour by the window, wishing she had been more forceful in persuading Malcolm to delay the onset of schooling, yet knowing he was right to insist and loving him as always for his decisiveness. The regret subsided under the soothing words of psalms read half aloud and then the busy work of fingers and needle at the crochet pattern. Silly and selfish, she told herself. There was still plenty of time left in the week for play and walks and carriage rides and splashing about at the riverside.

The truly painful test came when the boy was fourteen, now taller than Melissa, and ready—even eager—to leave for the preparatory school that Malcolm had decreed and that she had accepted with outward serenity. What choice was there? She closed her mind to futile imagining that Savannah had a proper school for him; it simply didn't and so they would take him to Augusta, one hundred and ten miles away, and leave him there.

She took what comfort she could from knowing that the priest who headmastered the school was an old seminary friend of Malcolm's, the students were carefully chosen, the classrooms and living quarters were roomy and comfortable, the busy Savannah river flowed between the two cities like a lifeline and there would be frequent visits back and forth.

The Marble King and Other Stories

I'm sure you're wondering if Malcolm remained stony and dogmatic through all this. On the way back from depositing the boy, they stood together on the steamer's rear deck when it left the Augusta pier. Although Malcolm shunned public exhibitions as clearly unsuitable for a man wearing a clerical collar, on this day he astonished Melissa by suddenly slipping his arm around her waist and pulling her close until they were downriver and the city was well out of view.

The choice for college, four years later, was obvious for a lad so promising: William and Mary, the jewel of Southern universities, obvious, yes, but in Virginia, six hundred miles away, with visits measured in months, not weeks.

They held hands tightly, Malcolm and Melissa, returning in a railroad car too crowded for any other display, Malcolm telling her repeatedly that William and Mary's divinity school was the ideal place for their son, naming the renowned faculty members who would be teaching him, proclaiming over and over how gifted a boy must be in order to qualify until Melissa brushed his cheek with a finger and they rode on in quiet.

After the first parting, four years earlier, Melissa had filled her calendar with women's meetings and luncheons and charity visits, carefully leaving gaps for time in the wingback chair. Now, she placed a Book of Common Prayer beside the psalm book in the attic and spent more hours there, meditating, *connecting*, than before. She took Malcolm Junior's letters also—he was that rare youth who wrote home faithfully—and she held them to the light, reading, re-reading and *handling* the sheets of paper. She would manage this new separation, she told herself.

With daily resolution she did, but by Malcolm junior's final year she was like a spring uncoiling, busily planning the homecoming party two months in advance. More, forcing herself to be realistic about her son's age, she started to assess the mar-

The Wingback Chair

riageable young women of Savannah, trying to imagine one worthy of him.

These daydreams would shatter, along with millions of others, for the year was 1861 and the month was April. I know you will immediately picture the twelfth day of that month, the violently idiotic day when secessionists fired at Fort Sumter.

The message from Malcolm Junior was hasty and brief. The college would arrange a brevet lieutenant's commission in a Virginia cavalry unit so he could start training immediately, rather than lose time coming home to pursue a Georgia appointment. He would keep them informed.

He did, sketchily. Assigned to General Longstreet's corps, present at Bull Run, Second Bull Run, promoted to Captain, then on to Suffolk and Gettysburg, promoted to Major, on to Chattanooga and there the letters stopped. They had never contained battle details, deliberately, of course, but the very names smelled of smoke and blood, and the promotions told of risks taken, personal safety ignored, everything they expected, everything they dreaded.

The Chattanooga letter was dated November, 1863. Malcolm paced the vicarage rooms, writing inquiries with no mail system to carry them, planning trips to Chattanooga made impossible with the railroads crippled and Sherman's implacable army on the march. They shared fearful nights of prayer, Melissa sometimes taking the lead, the instigator for the first time in their marriage, giving reassurance to Malcolm and a sense of purpose to herself.

They were sitting on the veranda one August evening in 1864 when a constable brought them a visitor, a skeletal young man in a heavily patched sergeant's uniform. He had been asking in town for the Reverend Witherspoon.

The Marble King and Other Stories

Sweet tea served, faces invisible in the growing dusk, Malcolm and Melissa heard the sergeant's story of his escape from the Union army prison camp at Point Lookout, Maryland, where Major Witherspoon had been shipped after being wounded and captured at Chattanooga, and where he had died last month.

In answer to Malcolm's question, he said Yes, he had been present, there was no doubt, I'm so sorry, Reverend.

Melissa held on for three weeks.

It's that lifelong condition of hers, said the doctor, writing cardiac arrest in Latin on the death certificate, there being no medical term for brokenhearted mother.

The bishop came to conduct the funeral and the Sunday services while Malcolm sat rigid in a pew. He sat the same way in the vicarage parlor for a few days, intoning barely audible gratitude to those from the congregation and the city who came to call.

By the following Sunday, he was again in the pulpit, preaching with the same power and lucidity as before, although a suggestion of harshness crept into his voice from time to time. In church meetings and visits, the more observant congregants caught an occasional clenching of hands or silent tapping of feet.

A housekeeper was found, a stocky and white-haired woman named Mrs. Finch who, in common with every efficient housekeeper, examined the house carefully on the first day, *all* of the house.

Descending from the attic, she asked Malcolm if he wanted to keep everything stored there.

"I don't know what's there. My wife took care of such things."

"Well, much of it is useful and might be sold or given to charity," said Mrs. Finch with delicacy. "We could have tradesmen in to look it over, except for the pretty little chair the missus used for prayer and her crocheting. That's too nice to part with, I should think."

<hr />

Malcolm stood over the chair, visualizing, comprehending. There were no detectable tears but people handle these things differently, as you know. Assume with me there were inward tears of discovery, of guilt, of yearning and of joy, yes, joy, at this unexpected gift.

The wingback went into his study, next to his oversized reading chair, the place where he spent his most private hours. He kept the books, the crochet patterns and letters on the little chair, exactly as he found them. He shifted his own chair so the wingback could easily be seen when he looked up from a page. That's as far as he went, so you needn't fret about the chair becoming a shrine and the scene descending into melodrama. Malcolm, after all, was a priest and he knew that objects are not to be worshipped.

Nevertheless, he marveled at the way this bit of wood and fabric had metamorphosed into a hidden symbol of resistance and then into a sanctuary for prayer, patience and renewal. He contemplated the little wingback, trying to remember just where it had been among the ornate furnishings, able to recall only the personal sermon he had delivered to Melissa about simplicity, more nervous than he revealed—preaching to your bride is not taught in seminary—but certain that a clergyman must take the lead in marriage just as he did in church.

He left the vicarage for St. Thomas, avoiding the chancel door, walking to the public entrance instead. He knelt in the back row and prayed for over an hour.

It was not long before parishioners noticed that visits were different. When Malcolm came to call, or when they went to the vicarage, he lingered over the coffee and little plum cakes with-

The Marble King and Other Stories

out checking the clock, chatting on with them about the weather and their children and their gardens and how lovely the parks and riverside looked again, now that Sherman was gone.

The suggestion of harshness in Malcolm's voice disappeared, the clenching hands and restless feet also. The Sunday messages were subtly different. One deacon asked another if there weren't more references to Psalms these days.

At church meetings about the scheduling of events or the allotment of funds or the perpetual disagreements over choir selections, more opinions were heard, even encouraged. Eventually, Malcolm would propose a logical solution, just as before, but absent the glint in the eye.

Said an older member to his wife, "He's the same Reverend Witherspoon. I mean there's no doubt who's in charge, except it's, well, easier."

"He listens more," she said.

The congregation, which had always admired Reverend Witherspoon, the priest, now began to appreciate Malcolm Witherspoon, the man. It was common to hear people praise God for the way He can pull a good work out of a terrible tragedy.

Sophisticate that you are, you'll shrug that off, I know.

So will I, after a while.

James plays piano.

Freda plays violin.

They perform concert duets together in perfect harmony.

Alright, almost perfect…

Dialogue In D flat

"He's signaling OK, good cut, can you believe it?"
"Why not? It *was* a good cut."
"Freda, please. That discord–fourteenth bar?"
"No discord. Artistic dissonance."
"Artistic? It's a mistake. Shaganowsky never wrote it that way."
"Don't be dogmatic, James. Those original manuscripts of Shaganowsky's were a mess. Who knows if he meant D flat or D natural?"
"A century and a half of musical history knows! Nobody ever played that note flat. There was simply a mistake in the violin part of the new transcription."
"Then why does a mistake sound so interesting?"
"To a stubborn violinist, interesting. To a true musical ear, dissonance– "
"Every great composer used dissonance, Vivaldi, Hayden, Bach– "

The Marble King and Other Stories

"Don't treat me like an idiot. They used it deliberately, not because some copyist's finger slipped—"

"Shhh, James. He's signaling for the next movement."

"Signals, lights, dials. I hate recording studios. No applause, no partnership with an audience."

"Yes, but such perfect sound quality."

"To immortalize a mistake, pfah!"

"Light's on. Stop crabbing and give me a beat."

"Why did you tell the cab to go through the park instead of straight up West End? We would have been home sooner and cheaper."

"The park is more interesting."

"On a rainy, foggy day when you can't even see a tree? Oh, I get it. *Interesting.* Very subtle, James. You've got the emotional maturity of an eight year old. How long are you going to sulk about that D flat?"

"Looking concerned is not sulking. We're doing the Shaganowsky live next week at Carnegie. What then?"

"Actually, the park is interesting in the fog and rain. The trees have that ghostly, dissonant shape, don't you think?"

"Like I said last week, the emotional maturity of an eight year old."

"Freda, we're going straight up West End this time. What's the problem?"

"Stop the smirking, James. You know the problem: that D major chord."

"Problem? I played it exactly as Shaganowsky wrote it, a simple D major."

16

"You didn't play it. You steam-hammered it! Shaganowsky never put a fortissimo there."

"No, it's mezzo forte, which leaves room for interpretation, so I played it just a bit louder, an *artistic* interpretation."

"A childish interpretation, to drown out my D flat. You might have ruined the whole sonata."

"Ruined it? My love, I'm the one trying to preserve its integrity."

"Don't *my love* me. And you can't do that fortissimo next week at Aspen. You know how sound reverberates outdoors."

"I might bring on rain."

"James! I'm serious."

"It's up to you, my love."

"Freda, you've gone mad! You can't upset the tempo. It's beyond devious, which I expect from you by now. It's just outrageous."

"A little quarter note ahead, piffle, and it sounded quite creative."

"A little sneak attack, slipping ahead of my chord, and you'll notice, *my love*, you never had to do it. I played the chord at its traditional level. I did not try to bury your silly D flat."

"Stop being so self-righteous. You were afraid of the outdoor acoustics..........James?"

"What?"

"You're just sitting. Nothing to say?"

"Sorry. My mind was wandering to that decimal point, you remember—"

"Oh! Talk about a sneak attack! That was two years ago, everything is straightened out, and it had nothing to do with our music."

"Metaphorically, it did, and does. The decimal point, the D flat, do you see the connection?"

"No! The decimal point was an innocent mistake."

The Marble King and Other Stories

"Ah, we're getting to the point. Mistakes have consequences, and they can be long-lasting. How long did it take us to get our finances back under control?"

"You're impossible, James. And a terrible ingrate. You were tied up on the Mendelssohn orchestration, the agency needed an accounting, so I tried to help. Any mature man would be forgiving."

"I did forgive you, I do forgive you, always will forgive you. We're at the real point now. An innocent mistake, as you say, in something where you had no experience, poof, it happens. But you are an experienced musician—"

"Thank you."

"—so clinging to this D flat mistake is forcing me into some desperate actions—"

"Actually, you've been quite inventive."

"—and you know I don't like flamboyance."

"Oh? Like the day of the Baldwin? No flamboyance there? I will not play the Knabe, you said. I must have the Baldwin. Otherwise I will not perform."

"Freda! How can you possibly compare—and to bring that up after all these years—that was a matter of absolute artistic integrity."

"That was a matter of a twenty-one year old student pianist letting a couple of minor triumphs inflate his head like a balloon. Imagine, an ultimatum to the manager of Tanglewood, the most prominent music festival of the summer, from a student playing a workshop performance."

"Minor triumphs? Minor triumphs? They were the best reviewed performances in years."

"In the university newspaper. Not quite The New York Times, *my love*. It took you a whole year, as I recall, to get your performance schedule renewed."

"With my artistic integrity unsullied. And, as I recall, *my love*, you cheered when I insisted on the Baldwin and even cried when they cancelled me."

"An eighteen year old girl with a silly crush on a temperamental pianist, something out of a Victorian novel."

"A novel turned real, you must admit. Those girlish dreams that the temperamental pianist would invite you to play duets with him some day—"

"You invited? The agency scheduled us together, and only because we were accidentally available at the same time."

"I accepted you, the same thing."

"After the Baldwin experience, you were accepting anything the agency asked."

"Stop revising history! I had a New York Times review by then and it was excellent."

"So did I, James. You must admit that."

"Except it didn't warn me of the stubborn streak that would someday ruin a great sonata and bring me such heartache and unremitting distress."

"Oh, good. We're both in the Victorian novel now. What will your unremitting distress make you do in Pittsburgh Saturday night? We're back indoors there."

"I'll do whatever is needed to preserve our reputation. One of us has to act responsibly."

"The thirty-fourth bar? James, really, a crescendo in the thirty fourth bar?"

"It's a repeat of the fourteenth. When you extended your disastrous D flat *after* the chord in the fourteenth, I mean, it was bad enough when you slipped it in *before* the chord at Aspen, but tonight, holding it *after* the chord, throwing the piano harmony into chaos—"

"You recovered beautifully, James, that sly little G flat to slide us back in."

"Of course, I did. I always rise to the challenge. That's why I crescendoed in the thirty-fourth, a pre-emptive strike against your repeating your criminally childish action in the fourteenth. Freda! Stop giggling! I am not a violent man, but—"

"Yes, you'll break a thirty-thousand dollar Guarnieri violin over my head. Now then, seriously, James, we have to think about next week. Lincoln Center, with PBS there, live national TV, those cameras picking up every expression—"

"And that antiseptic hall, the operating room lighting, couldn't they at least have put a chandelier in the place, a portrait or two on the walls—"

"I know, I know, but no point moaning, and it is our biggest event of the year, maybe even in our career, so?"

"So, with the cameras examining our fingernails and the microphones magnifying every speck of sound, picking up harmonics we're not even aware of, James and Freda play traditional Shaganowsky, direct from 1878, no extra little problems to rattle us, are we in tune here?"

"We are."

"Ah, Freda, you're home finally."

"Finally? I've been out thirty minutes to get some groceries and the Times."

"Yes, yes, well, I'm impatient because the mail came and because Sam at the agency called. I have some things to tell you—"

"And I have something to tell you."

"—first, the mail brought the latest issue of Classical Scene and here, page four, I quote, Please take note of an inadvertent error in the new transcription of the Shaganowsky Piano and Violin Sonata: fourteenth bar, the violin D flat should be D natural. The transcription service offers apologies for any inconvenience. Unquote. You might want to do as much, *my love*. Freda? Are you smiling? It's hardly amusing."

"No, not at all, James. You said Sam called?"

"He read Classical Scene and wondered if we wanted to re-do the first movement in the recording. I told him yes, we'll record it correctly this time. Freda? You are smiling. I think you're laughing."

"No, no. Or just a little. Let me get it under control. I have some reading to do, too, from today's New York Times. Owen Epps reviewed our concert last night."

"Epps himself? Not one of the second-stringers?"

"Epps himself, the most influential music critic of our generation, professor of classical composition at Harvard, author of nineteen books, five-time winner of the Music History Award, the man who can make or break a musician's career—"

"Are you reviewing Epps or is he reviewing us? You're deliberately toying with me, Freda."

"The headline is, Impeccable Shaganowsky Performance Offered By Mauriano and Gilbert."

"Impeccable? I see why you're smiling."

"Not yet, you don't. Here's what he writes. Quote. The piano and violin duo of James Mauriano and Freda Gilbert (Mr. and Mrs. in private life) brought an impeccable performance of the Shaganowsky Piano and Violin Sonata to a rapt Lincoln Center audience last night. The two artists were clearly in a traditional frame of mind and from the very first note they built an epic performance so purely classical the austerely modern NYC auditorium was transformed into the rococo splendor of Vienna's Golden Hall, site of the work's 1878 premiere. Bouquets from this reviewer to Mr. Mauriano's powerful and precise piano and Ms. Gilbert's soaring and melodic violin. Unquote. Well now, James, aren't you pleased?"

"The right choice, Freda, my love, the right choice to go traditional. Don't second guess the great composers."

"Never, my love. There's more from Epps, listen. I quote. However......"

"However?"

"However........"

"However what? He's already given us a rave notice. He can't possibly spoil it."

"Not for me, James. I quote. However, in the back of one's mind was the couple's recent adventurous approach to the Shaganowsky work. Although revealed now as a transcriber's error, a D flat in the fourteenth bar was boldly used by Mr. Mauriano and Ms. Gilbert for a welcome flight of fancy in their recent appearances, reawakening and reenergizing the sonata. Reports from around the music world have excitedly told of the unexpected touch of artistic dissonance from Ms. Gilbert's strings in a recording session, a fortissimo from Mr. Mauriano's piano in a concert, a tempo caprice from Ms. Gilbert in the next concert, and most recently, an absolutely unprecedented thirty-fourth bar crescendo from the piano, all of it taking this sometimes too predictable piece into an imaginative new realm. Without diminishing one's praise for last night's performance, one confesses to an *appetit* for the pair to go on astonishing us. Mr. Mauriano's piano, deep and varied as the ocean tides, and Ms. Gilbert's violin, swooping sweet and free as a lark in flight, ah, where could they not transport us? Unquote."

DIALOGUE IN D FLAT

"Fmmmmpt."

"James? You're muttering."

"Where could they not transport us—to acceptable performances, that's where."

"Think about Epps, James. Careers blossom when you follow his *appetits* and they seem to vanish when you don't."

"I will not allow our lives to be swayed by a critic. Of course, he did say powerful and precise piano, deep and varied as the ocean tides...those are memorable compliments, you know."

"James?"

"What? Oh yes, of course, my love, soaring and melodic violin, sweet and free as a lark in flight. It's possible now that we could play London, the Royal Festival Hall; Paris, the Elysee; Rome, the Parco Della Musica—"

"Think Vienna, the Golden Hall. Mauriano and Gilbert bring the Shaganowsky sonata back to its birthplace in a daring new conception."

"Dazzling and daring. No, no, deep and dazzling and daring. You know, Freda, after dinner, or maybe even before, we might re-examine the second movement, the piano triplets passage, there are possibilities with the rhythm—let me call Sam first, he must have seen the Times by now......

......Sam, it's James...yes, we just read it...well, we're thinking international tour...I know, naturally, the recording will be vital... no, no, we'll forget traditional and follow Epps, bring in all the fresh new ideas we've been experimenting with, the fortissimos, the crescendo, and the F natural I used in the last concert—I could expand that into a little *fantasia* with the violin...Freda? Oh, no problem at all, she can be adaptable, she'll be fine with it, she's right here, saying something—what, my love? You're mumbling, could you speak a little louder...ah, yes, she says she'll be just fine with it.

It's alright to share painful personal problems with a stranger on a train, as long as it's the Adirondack Express, the day is sunny, and Lake Champlain is blue and sparkly…

Witnesses

God places the brightest ideas in large bodies of water. For example, ride north along the Hudson for three hundred miles and then go another hundred along Lake Champlain, so wide its far shore is often a mystery, and ideas that would stay buried under the weight of land rise up like winged seraphim from the waves. Once you become aware of them, you think, *Well, of course!*

One such idea, as brash as it was obvious, came to Reverend Richard Baum, pastor of Heritage Baptist Church in Croton, and to his traveling companion, Daniel Pittman, a Pace University graduate student, at the same instant. No words were spoken; none were needed. They simply kept staring at the diamond wavelets cresting Champlain, knowing the idea was now *here*, like the lake, too big to be wished away, and clearly His work.

They had met five hours ago. The reverend boarded Amtrak's Adirondack line in Croton. He carried an overnight bag and a

The Marble King and Other Stories

small red and white cooler to a seat in the café car. Thanksgiving travelers crowded the train and the seat facing him across a tiny service table was one of the few vacant spots left.

At the next stop, Poughkeepsie, the remaining places were filled by people who simply dropped into them, except for Daniel, who stood at the seat by the reverend and asked, "May I?"

"Please," came the friendly answer, although the reverend was surveying Daniel in the inwardly wary manner one does when thrown together with a stranger. Daniel, naturally, did the same toward the reverend.

Each was pleased.

Daniel, by the easy smile of the somewhat portly, fiftyish man who faced him and by the way his freshly pressed suit and well barbered face was contradicted by an uncombed, spiky fringe of grey hair. Conventional, yes, but with a dash of free spirit.

Reverend Baum, by Daniel's inquisitive eyes behind somewhat old fashioned horn rimmed glasses, by the cleanliness of his turtleneck sweater and jeans, and by the prominent sticker on a gym bag Daniel set down by the seat. Got Jesus? it asked. Obviously a well bred young man but with a touch of boldness.

"Yes is the answer," said Reverend Baum, gesturing at the sticker. "I usually ask that question myself in one form or another."

"I'm not surprised. You're a pastor, aren't you?"

"What gave it away?"

"What I call the ministerial smile. There's a certain humility to it, yet it says, 'I know something you must hear.'"

"I thought I smiled that way only when saying, 'In conclusion.'"

"You mean when the sermon still has fifteen minutes to go?"

"I usually aim for twenty."

Mischievous grins came from both sides and conversation flowed naturally then, the ever-joyful conversation between born-again Christians discovering each other. From exchanging salvation stories to gently debating Predestination, from questioning the popularity of Christian rock music to praising God's sovereignty in all things, the talk rolled as serenely as the river beside them.

Each had a missionary story to tell. For the reverend, it was his year-long break from pastoring to teach at a Bangladeshi missions school in the teeming, claustrophobic slums of the capital, Dhaka.

Were souls saved?

Yes, praise God, by the dozens.

For Daniel, it was the year between his bachelor's degree in Information Systems and the start of graduate work. Given a choice between internship in the Tampa highway bureau and a church-building mission in Liberia, he chose Liberia. Plenty of sunshine either way, he joked.

Did he build a church?

Three of them, with the Lord's help.

He looked across the river, at hills topped by the skeletal tree line of late November. "Three of them," he repeated. "Do I sound self-righteous about it?"

Thirty years in ministry had taught Reverend Baum that certain questions were like gates opening. "Why would you ask that?" he prompted.

Daniel still watched the river. The reverend waited. Finally, Daniel replied, "I'm going all the way to Plattsburgh, the last stop before Canada. I spend the holiday there every year with my cousin and his wife, supposedly for Thanksgiving dinner, in truth to be God's witness to them."

Reverend Baum blinked twice at that, as if faintly startled, a look that came and went swiftly.

"They tell me I'm self righteous," Daniel continued. He turned to face the reverend now. "They could be right. I'm sure I come

The Marble King and Other Stories

off that way but I'm simply not one of your quiet persuaders."
He pointed at the Got Jesus? sticker.

"More power to you," Reverend Baum said. "And even if you
talk quietly, the people you're closest to are the quickest to call
you self-righteous. First cousins?"

"First cousins, the same age, grew up in a two family house,
playmates since the diaper stage, even resemble each other—our
mothers were sisters—and we were brothers in our own eyes."

"But growing up together—one a believer, the other not?"

"Churchgoers together, baptized together, Sunday school together, Christian school together, believers together, until the
senior year of high school. His parents were coming home from
an evening prayer meeting. They stopped to help a young couple
whose car was off the road—"

"Oh?" interrupted the reverend. "Six years ago? That was
your family?"

"The Good Samaritan murders the papers called it, yes. For my
aunt's quarter-carat ring, my uncle's Timex watch and fourteen
dollars. It shook my faith for a little while but it totally destroyed
Steven's. 'They were trying to help,' he kept saying."

"He came to live with you then?"

"Yes, grim and depressed, but we thought he was hanging on
until we were forced to rent out the other half of the house. No
way to afford it all any more. It was a side by side affair, with an
archway between that we would flow through, back and forth.
We had to wall it off now. Steven and I came home from school
and there was my dad at work. The sheet rock was already nailed
in place." Daniel paused, remembering.

"I started to help," he resumed in a moment. "Dad was taping
by then. Steven stood there as if paralyzed, watching the last
little cracks of light disappear under the tape. I went to stand
by him, put my arm around him. Steven pushed me away, hard."

Daniel removed his glasses and wiped a hand over his eyes. "I know all of us in the room missed my uncle terribly just then. He was older than my dad by about ten years, a father figure and the listener in the family, the sweetest-tempered of men, and he could make anger or resentment evaporate when he walked into a room." Daniel took a slow breath and finished, "Steven watched until we were done, then walked into town and enlisted in the air force. He had just turned eighteen, no family permission needed."

The faintly startled look came and went again as Reverend Baum said, "But he stayed in touch, obviously."

"He hasn't returned to the house since then but he emails and telephones. Materially, things worked out well. He was trained by the air force in helicopter maintenance so the state police hired him for their helicopters when he was discharged. High pay, full benefits, a pension. He has a lovely wife, a baby six months old, a nice home, all the good things."

"Meaning you're preaching to the contented, very hard to do. His wife, though, is she receptive?"

"She comes from a family of atheists, probably one of her attractions for him. She politely recites Schopenhauer and Kant when I quote scripture. Steven has learned to do that, too. Not politely," he added.

"So there are scenes. Impatient with each other as only brothers can be."

"Like a reflex at this point. It's been that way for four years now. I keep trying." Daniel laughed without humor. "Is that perseverance? Or does it fit the definition of stupidity: doing the same thing over and over and expecting a different result?"

The reverend let a few seconds go by. "Let's call it perseverance," he said quietly. His eyes roamed around the car and came to rest on the empty service table between them. "Some coffee?"

He stood quickly as if needing the movement and led the way to the beverage stand. Daniel said, "I've imposed my trouble on you, haven't I? It was impulsive and I apologize."

"I encouraged it. A pastor who can't hear about someone's trouble needs a new line of work."

Daniel placed a cup under the spigot as Reverend Baum continued, "Actually, I was listening to you with much more than a pastor's ear. It was personal for me from the start, deeply so. I assume neither of us believes in coincidence?"

Daniel released the lever, halting the flow. He raised his hand in a slow, exaggerated motion and brought it down to restart the spigot.

"Exactly. For all things, even a simple cup of coffee, a moving hand, an ultimate purpose. So here's something to consider: I'm getting off at Port Kent, the next station. An old friend lives there. He's a man who also lost his family and lost his faith with it. Like you, I go to witness to him year after year and like you, I return feeling defeated."

Daniel was passing the cup to the reverend and his hand stopped in mid-air. "And here we are," he said, pointedly watching his hand. "Same train, same car, seated together."

Settled by the window again, Reverend Baum leaned toward Daniel. "My first pastorate was in Port Kent. I made friends quickly with a fellow my age, Nathan Simms, raising a three year old son by himself. His wife ran off a year earlier. Not a good marriage from the start. I'm told she was a gorgeous girl but something of a high school celebrity, for all the wrong reasons. As for Nathan, well, his yearbook entry was 'Church going guy, never tells a lie.'"

"Why would she be interested in him? Money?"

"An over-familiar story, isn't it? Nathan's family was wealthy, at least by the standards of a small town. His grandfather had picked up several acres of lakeside property in the Depression, when you could buy it for pennies. After World War Two there was money again and families came from Burlington, Albany, Syracuse, even Montreal, to vacation on Champlain. Nathan's father built rental cottages on the property. They fill nearly a mile of prime shoreline." He sipped at his coffee and peered at Daniel over the rim. "Summer cottages on Champlain attract a rich crowd, big city rich."

Daniel frowned. "You said she ran off."

"Without a word, except for divorce papers from an Albany law firm the next month."

"And he handled it badly?"

"There's a cottage away from the rest, on a little rise a few hundred yards inland. The family built it for themselves. He holed up there, just himself and Matthew, the little boy. He returned to his house and his business after a week, but so nervous he could hardly talk until the divorce papers arrived. Then he called me, all excited, and said, 'Richard, this woman is so faithless, she's even indifferent to her son. The settlement gives me sole custody without even asking for visiting rights. Matthew is mine to raise.' He actually laughed."

Daniel stared into his coffee cup, then asked, "Did he ever marry again?"

The question brought an appreciative look from the reverend. "You're quick to grasp a situation. No, he played mother and father to the boy, barely letting him out of his sight. He hired a manager for the rental business, so he had time to cook, shop, play, even home school the boy until Matthew was twelve and demanded regular schooling. He tore his books into shreds when Nathan refused. Nathan relented and sent him to a Christian academy, although he drove the boy back and forth—wouldn't

The Marble King and Other Stories

allow a school bus—and bombarded the staff with phone calls and unannounced visits to make certain Matthew was alright."

"I'm sure you told him to give the boy some room."

"I had been called to the Croton church by then. A much bigger congregation, more prestige, but sometimes—" He shrugged and continued, "Like you and your cousin, phone and email kept us in touch. Predictably, Matthew became a problem. Failing grades, disruptive in class, screaming arguments at home. In his junior year, he was arrested for shoplifting, then narcotics. Good lawyers got him off with probation and public service. It seemed to straighten him out. He spoke very little but when he did it was courteous. He did his public service well, attended classes, earned his diploma, even filled out the application Nathan brought home from the community college, three miles away. Then, the morning he was eighteen, he did what your cousin did, except he chose the navy."

Daniel shook his head. "That means your friend was rejected a second time. The wife, then the son. How did he handle this one?"

"Nathan sent letters to boot camp daily, sent packages of food even though it was against the rules, showed up before breakfast on graduation day, the first time a visit was permitted. Matthew was polite, agreeable to everything his father asked, promised to go to college when his tour was over. Nathan sounded uneasy when he told me about it, and he was right."

The reverend tipped his head back to drain the coffee cup and leaned close again.

"Matthew was assigned to the Mediterranean fleet. When they docked in Trieste, he jumped ship. The navy informed Nathan his son had disappeared and was listed as a deserter. Nathan went to Trieste and hired an investigator. The man tracked Matthew to Rome and gave up. The boy could be anywhere in the world now, Signor.' Nathan spent a year in different European cities, hiring detective agencies, blindly walking boulevards and back streets himself, jumping at a glimpse of any young man at a bus stop, in a café, on a park bench."

The reverend spread his hands in a gesture of helplessness. Human folly, who can overcome it?

"He came home and sold his business, except for that isolated cottage, where he lives alone. He spends a lot of time fishing, a lot of time walking the shore, a lot of time simply looking out the front window. He owned a fine collection of Bibles and Christian reading, all at the bottom of the lake now."

"Does he listen when you witness to him?"

"Yes, calmly. He doesn't argue the way your cousin does. He says he understands why I have to do it, even teases me about it, says it's the price he has to pay for my wife's cooking."

The reverend bent to tap the cooler under the seat, then clasped the armrest for balance as the train rounded a sharp bend. A wider portion of the lake was now revealed, the far shore only a mist. The tracks descended to hug the waterside and both men fell silent, lost in the glinting blue vastness unexpectedly so close. Conversation had stilled in the rest of the car, as usual by late afternoon. The rhythmic clamor of the wheels underneath was the only sound for several miles until the train pulled away from the shore and the reverend said, "Do you have a pen?"

He had taken a yellow pad from his bag They looked at each other in perfect comprehension. The reverend tore off a page for Daniel and one for himself. They each wrote for a few minutes, then folded their papers. The reverend put Daniel's in his bag; Daniel slipped the reverend's into his shirt pocket. As if on cue, they bowed their heads, the reverend praying for Daniel's mission, Daniel for the reverend's.

The Marble King and Other Stories

The train slowed for the Port Kent station and the two men embraced and parted. A few moments later, a conductor walked excitedly to Reverend Baum and looked beneath his seat. "You had a red and white cooler when you got on, didn't you? Some young fellow has it now, up front there, about to get off with it." He pointed accusingly.

"Yes, I know. He has my ticket, too, and I have his. That's alright, isn't it? The fares are paid in any event."

The conductor let his arm drop. "Well, I don't see any problem for the railroad with that." He threw a puzzled look at the front of the car, then at Reverend Baum. "Guess you know what you're doing."

A minute later, the doors opened and Daniel stepped on the Port Kent platform. He patted the letter in his pocket, and looked for a taxi.

Thirty minutes more and Reverend Baum stepped off at Plattsburgh. He took the letter from his bag and looked around for a young man who resembled Daniel.

No kidding,
there was daily entertainment before TV and the Internet.
It was called the neighborhood…

Brownstone 1940

Personally, I preferred 3B for my sister. He had the tweed jacket, you know, with the elbow patches and a tweed cap and I knew he smoked a pipe although Madeleine, my sister, said it was in my imagination and she should know, she said, having spent time in a movie show sitting next to him and if he smoked anything she would smell it (she let him kiss her, I'll bet a Flyin' Jenny comic on it, which is how she knew, or thought she knew, better than me—I —); in any event, he had a certain *joie de vivre*—I love saying that ("You don't even know what it means!" Madeleine said) ("Elegance," I told her and she rolled her eyes, typical Madeleine) but it's her choice, boy friends, she's the one who's nineteen and I'm nine (a 'surprise' child, which I'm tired of hearing) and she did have to rearrange her room to cram me in (which I'm also tired of hearing; I mean, it's as crowded for me as it is for her, more even, since she's got a dressing table and hair sprays and lipstick and powders and such and drawers full of brassieres and garter belts and stuff that jams me into maybe two drawers and a little space on the floor for my school books—yes, she does help me with math, she's good at it, okay, the least she could do) but the fact is, she likes 1A better. She's even broken a date with 3B to go out with 1A, sort of risky with them living in the same brownstone and I think she enjoyed that, she has a little reckless side, once even came home after midnight when she was sixteen and Dad, who's a quiet fellow—Mom's louder, usually—but Dad, this time he yelled so the plates rattled and she never did that again until she turned eighteen and legally an adult, which we heard about *incessantly*—(vocabulary, English class, that's where I'm good, *exceptional*, Mr. Kirk, the principal, said) until Dad's voice went up a notch, not a yell but you knew it was there like a teacher waving the ruler above your knuckles, explaining that she still lived under his roof, ate the food he earned, and would live his rules, legal adult, pfooey, so Madeleine hugged Mom, who patted her back and looked at Dad with one of those "you don't understand girls" looks (I thought he understood me pretty well; never brought home any of the fancy millinery for me that he did for Mom and Madeleine from the lady's hat factory where he worked even though they made that frou-frou stuff for kids)—anyway, Madeleine stopped the legal adult talk.

She did stay out, though, as late as one a.m., and dated who—whom—she wanted, and more often than not, it was1A. Now 3B was a graduate student and an instructor at City College, in History, which was the closest thing to English, and he was obviously on his way to being a professor, writing books like professors do—I sighed every time I thought of it, actually writing books—and the tweeds and the patches and the pipe! let Madeleine deny it all she wants—all that, while 1A played the cello.

Now I am not a *Philistine*. Music gives wings to the mind, Mom says, something she remembered from school, and I like the records Madeleine plays on the Decca portable she squeezed into our limited room space—on my side, understand—there's Buddy Clark singing "I'll Dance at Your Wedding" and Ruth Etting singing "Body and Soul" and some symphonies, real ones, by Mozart and I like them; I listen to parts of them in the afternoon by myself sometimes, so let me explain this:

There's music, and there are musicians. Musicians, a cello player, anyway, says, "Hey kid, get the door," wearing a cracked leather jacket and no hat while he wrestles that case the size of a gorilla, a beat-up, peeling, moth-eaten gorilla, down the brownstone steps and on down the street to the subway.

Compare that with a graduate instructor in History who says, "Good morning, Janine. Any good compositions in there? (meaning my school books) I bet there are. Does the teacher have you read your work aloud?"

I told him about the time I used the words *vehemently* and *obtuse* in a read-aloud piece and my best friend, Rhoda, said I was a snob.

"You have to accept the Philistines (that's where I learned that word) to get on in the world. We're all God's children, you know. And Rhoda's nice, I'm certain, or you wouldn't be best friends, right?"

I told him she was, and anyway, it's easy to see what I mean: a real conversation, person to person, no Hey kid, get the door and besides, musicians don't seem to work when you expect. They're home, and you can see them going to the Rexall lunch counter in a stained sweat shirt, looking sleepy at three in the afternoon, ordering toast and coffee when you're getting a chocolate malt or something else normal, while History instructors are grading papers or even sneaking in some writing time on their books at that hour, in tweeds.

I will *concede* the sounds of cello practice are okay. Passing by 1A's door on the way in or out—first floor, you know, 1A—you can hear some nice sounds, the low notes rolling around, the high notes tingling your ears and once coming home after Library Club I caught Madeleine standing at the bottom of the stairs, a bag of groceries Mom was waiting for sitting on the floor, Madeleine just listening in sort of a trance so I poked her and she patted my head, no poke back, no pinch, only a pat, so I stayed with her, to let her know I got it, nine years old brings some *sophistication*—enough actually, to hope she knew this was a moment that would blow over, and that thinking lifetime, 3B was the better bet.

And guess what? 1A proved it with a loud sneeze followed by some really thunderous nose-honking that broke the minute all to pieces and Madeleine picked up the grocery bag and sort of flittered up the stairs while I backed up and waited for some clearance for a running start because charging up the stairs is one of the reasons for living in a brownstone, although not everyone knows most of them are not really brown colored stone (ours is), it's just a name that stuck from the first ones, which were really brown, and a person can walk from here to the river in Chelsea, like Rhoda and I do—that's our neighborhood, Chelsea, towards the lower end of Manhattan island by the Hudson—and see grey stone and white stone and a few tan and one painted yellow (bleh) but don't look for much brown, except if you go through the courtyard in General Theological Seminary on the way home from school, where the seminary buildings all around you are bricks but real brown with a teeny bit of maroon, so clean they must scrub them every night, while they have this really nice brown brick church, the Chapel of the Good Shepherd, where we go for the service on Easter and Christmas, but you can walk in any day and feel tiny under this high ceiling, I mean way above you, like the stars, and stare at the stained glass windows (with apostles and martyrs) that go all the way up, and the different ways the light comes through and the hush and echoes are all so magical that Rhoda, who's Jewish, says it's enough to make her believe Jesus really is the Messiah (she looks around as if her dad might hear) so the point here is that brownstone is really a type of house, not a color, three or four stories high, with steep concrete steps up to the front door, and they used to be private homes—mansions, really—but now are cut into apartments, six of them in our brownstone plus one in the basement for the super, some with one bedroom and some with two (which really could use three) but when you come in the front door it's like the old private home—except for the mailboxes—a large room with scrolled wood ledges in the walls and raised wood strips called *wainscoting* and scalloped borders at the ceiling, and this wide, wide staircase that sweeps upstairs in a big curve so you can charge top speed up and down until some grownup pops out with a *dyspeptic* look and makes you stop.

One time at Rhoda's brownstone we had four—us two—we two—and her neighbors, Roy and Bobby, and we charged up and made every door pop open and there was the biggest commotion (and Rhoda lost her allowance for that week but I shared mine with her) and also all the smells, one more thing to know about a brownstone, you can smell the cooking sort of all the time but when doors open all around, you can just about taste sausage and peach pie and meatloaf and pickled carp and a chicken roasting—I told Rhoda I'd do it all the time if she could afford it, which she thought was only a little bit funny.

But the outside steps were a different thing, which is another important point I'm getting to, those outside steps to the front door, concrete, eleven of them, smooth and worn, and even with a careful super who salts them in the morning like ours,

The Marble King and Other Stories

Gus, does, you have to go up or down like a mountain goat in a Natural Science class film, this foot, then that foot, hoof, and if you don't hold tight—did I say it's February, with ice, I'm telling about?—to the railing, you'll *plummet* right to the sidewalk.

And with a cello case? So, *predictably*, 1A went down, moth-eaten case went down, all with a terrible clatter and yell, which I heard and saw because I was coming back from buying the Daily News for Dad and here's the unlucky part: 3B was on the steps behind 1A and when 1A looked up, cello case on top of him and saw 3B looking down at him, he hollered, "What a cheap shot, shoving a fellow! You rotter! I'll take care of you!" And so he slid himself to his feet and made fists at 3B, who held up his hands and said, "You're wrong, you know, you simply—"

But 1A had swung at him by then and they were fighting, sort of, I mean holding each other and wrestling around like third grade boys in the schoolyard, nothing like Randolph Scott in a Saturday matinee sending a bad guy over the fence with one punch, but it was astounding enough to see grownup men in front of your own house on your own street doing such a thing and I was pushing at their knees or their backs, whatever I could reach as they whirled around, and swatting at them with the Daily News, trying to keep from getting trampled—later, when I thought about it, I got really scared and trembly—yelling, "Mr. Jikorsky, listen to me, Mr. Gramley didn't push you, he was way behind you, stop, stop, he never touched you!"

Oh.

Yes, I knew their names all along, this needs explaining: when I was very little and couldn't say the names of our neighbors, Dad, who sometimes gets *whimsical*, taught me to tell them apart by their apartment numbers, so the Bogulubovs (you see why I had trouble) became 2B and the Macillenys 3A and so on, and

42

even when I could say their names, the numbers stayed stuck in my head, okay?

There are always lots of people on a Chelsea street and men came running to stop the fight and to ask if I was alright and what in the world did you think you were doing, girlie? so I was able to be heard finally by Mr. Jikorskey who said, still a little *belligerent*, ""Yeah? Alright. Sorry." The 'sorry' was to Mr. Gramley, who said politely, "No damage. Misunderstanding, that's all."

He picked up some books he had dropped, said, "Thank you, gentlemen" to the others and "Thank you, Janine," to me with a slight bow and he walked off like Errol Flynn in The Dawn Patrol.

Mr. Jikorskey opened his case, which may have been ratty on the outside but was all soft, cushiony red stuff inside to hug the cello, which he looked over and kind of *massaged* and was satisfied and he closed up and said, mumbled, "Yeah, thanks," to everybody, pointed a finger at me, which I guess was a thank-you and *slouched* off. Well, maybe he walked off, but nobody would mistake him for Errol Flynn.

Except that it didn't matter how anybody walked because the harm had been done, and I mean real harm since those people who saw the fight from the other side of the street or through a window, not close where they could hear what really happened, told themselves and everybody else whose ear they could bend that the two men were fighting over Madeleine, with the clear meaning, What kind of girl is she, to encourage men to act like animals about her!

I had to suffer hearing it all through school the next day and even though Rhoda helped and so did the others who know I don't lie—not about something like this—the story grew every time it came to me: Jan, were they really all bloody and bruised? I hear Mr. Gramley's in the hospital, is Madeleine sorry for what

43

she did—that was the hardest of all, and I've never been so angry and I got hoarse telling people my sister did nothing wrong, but I didn't hit anybody except later in my *fantasies* because I'm self controlled and the real sufferer, of course, was Madeleine although maybe not all that much.

"Don't get so upset about it, Jan. It's a little funny in its way. And Mom and Dad understand gossip. By tomorrow, all the old hens will have something else to cackle about."

I stayed awake stewing about it while Madeleine fell asleep right away so I had to believe her, mostly, maybe not altogether because she stopped going out with both 3B and 1A from then on so the fight may have done something after all. Even though we live together, in one small room—well, I've made that point—she's old enough now to be mysterious at times like every other grownup.

So different boys, men, started showing up at the door for Madeleine, men she met at work—she got a job first try after high school, typing in what they call the Student Records office of New York University, *swarming* with college students and instructors and young professors and there was Madeleine, how she ever got any typing done I don't know—actually, she's so pretty that even out of the office, I mean with Mom and Dad and me around, she draws boys, men, like the day at the piers when the Queen Elizabeth, the Queen Mary and the Normandy were all docked side by side by side, the world's three largest liners at once, which I won't try to describe because there's a conversation that will do it better between my Dad and a sailor who somehow got through the crowd to Dad's side, although his eyes kept going flick, flick, at Madeleine and she knew it because she bent down and started asking me stupid things like Aren't they huge? Would you like to take an ocean cruise? and such to let the sailor know she had no interest in him (he was really cute, with crew cut hair, and tall, and wide shoulders and a white, starched uniform with those bell bottoms and USN pins on his collar for U.S. Navy) and he was telling Dad, they all do better than thirty nautical knots, as fast as his cruiser, the USS Helena –

"Thirty-five miles an hour," Dad said to show he knew about nautical knots.

"Right you are, sir," the sailor answered, "right you are, your husband's no amateur"—that was to Mom—"your dad knows his stuff, right?" to Madeleine and me and since Madeleine suddenly was looking at something interesting elsewhere, I answered, "Yes, sir."

"Pulls over eighty thousand tons, each one of them," Dad went on, then, to Mom and me—Madeleine was still elsewhere—and to show off a bit for the sailor, he said, "They're each about one thousand feet long, which means if you could stand them on end, they'd be as tall as the Chrysler Building and almost as tall as the Empire State," and he craned his neck up at the sky and so did Mom and I—and now Madeleine, too, because this was something we could get hold of, we had all stood on the sidewalk looking up, up, up at those skyscrapers (when I read the Daily News later I knew where Dad had learned all this) and the sailor said, "Wow, imagine," although that might have been about Madeleine, too, who had decided to look at him and even let her mouth turn from a frown to something that was not a frown.

"Steam turbines do the job, that thirty-five miles an hour," the sailor said to Dad, eyes moving up and down Madeleine like—as if—she might be the Chrysler Building, needing to be measured.

"Well, you can build a steam turbine big as Gibralter if you want," Dad said, "but it's the reduction gears that really do the work."

"Hmmmph?" said the sailor in surprise. Although his eyes now played with Madeleine's eyes—I mean, she actually looked down,

The Marble King and Other Stories

shyly (Madeleine?)—he did talk to Dad. So, something else to explain: I said Dad worked at a lady's hat factory and what he was, was the machinery maven. That's one of those New York City vocabulary words, maven, meaning expert, and at a hat factory there's a machine for cutting the felt and a machine for stretching the felt and a machine for steaming the felt and a machine for starching the felt and a machine for pressing the felt and the same kind of machines for straw hats and more machines for cutting, stretching and curling ribbons, and sixteen sewing machines for the ladies who do the brims and attach the bows and toy birds and feathers and sequins and stuff. Dad keeps all those machines running and they pay him forty dollars a week, a good fifteen dollars more than most jobs because without him they couldn't make any hats, plus he helps out some of the smaller factories when he has time, for another ten or even fifteen dollars each week. (We're not supposed to know any of this, Madeleine and I; Dad and Mom keep money things to themselves but they were talking so low when I went to the bathroom one night I had to stop in the hall and listen.) When I told Madeleine and I asked why we didn't get a bigger apartment, she said Mom and Dad were probably saving any extra money for us, for our weddings and to leave to us when they die (Mom? Dad? Die?) or in case of some emergency and I should clam up anyway, Madeleine said, because she'd be getting married soon enough so what the point is, is this: Dad knows machinery and he and the sailor went into this talk about gears and drive shafts and tork? (*torque*, I looked it up) and such and you could tell the sailor was really interested but his mind never left Madeleine and to show us the size of something called a flange on the steering rods he lined up Madeleine and me, and with one hand on Madeleine's shoulder to mark one end, he pushed me about a yard away to mark the other, but still holding on to Madeleine as he explained how the flange balanced the steering, even rocking Madeleine back and forth in case we forgot what balance was.

She was actually smiling now and he asked for her name and address so he could get in touch if he came back this way—the USS Helena was leaving tomorrow—and she wrote it down for him. "I could send you a grass skirt," he said. "We're sailing to a base in Hawaii, Pearl Harbor."

She gave him that look that says, "You're being fresh but it's fun," and he grinned back and we wished him well and I said, *Bon Voyage*, getting that roll of the eyes from Madeleine. So to get back to the start of all this, Madeleine is pretty, *vivacious*, and most probably I'll have that room to myself soon enough, as she says, because the boys, men, came by in a parade, week after week. There was never a Saturday night at home for Madeleine, Fridays and Sunday afternoons, too.

I got to say hello when they came by and none of them was anything like 3B, Mr. Gramley, for elegance, and since 1A, Mr. Jikorski, had suddenly moved out, and a bald-headed man with a cane had moved in, there was no more brownstone competition for Mr. Gramley, and Madeleine was not talking about any of the men she was dating, which gave me a little hope, so one Saturday afternoon when Rhoda and I came back from one of our walks, and Mr. Gramley was coming down the stairs, I did something really *impulsive*.

"Hello, Professor Gramley," I said

"You're ahead of the academic world, Janine, it's still Mr. Gramley, but I do like the way professor sounds."

That was why I said it, to sort of soften him up, and I introduced Rhoda ("Ah, the charming best friend," he said and she just about melted) and then I said, "Could I ask you a question, kind of personal?"

"I'm willing to hear it," he said, sitting down on the wide bottom step.

We sat on each side of him and I said, jumping right in, "Wouldn't you like to go out with my sister again? Let's say I needed some help with my History homework and you could come to our apartment when Madeleine was there and the two of you would get to talking and she'd see how smart you are and handsome and everything, you know?"

He pulled a pipe from his pocket (I knew it!!) and after he sort of played with it, he said, "You're very kind and although you're remarkably intelligent, that little scheme—well, you're a bit young to understand why grownups may not, hmmm, click. Your sister is a lovely girl, just lovely, and we respect each other, like each other, but there are no real, um, personality bonds between us."

Rhoda said, "You'd like to marry a lady professor," and I could have killed her until I saw that she was on to something. "Not that Madeleine isn't smart," she said in a rush to me, "it's just, well—"

"Madeleine is a smart girl, indeed," Mr. Gramley said, "but you have the general idea about the two of us."

"I suppose so," I said. I think I sighed because I could tell it was no use. "I tried, and at least I don't have to worry about that creepy musician in 1A any more."

"Ah," he said, "Mr. Jikorsky. Did you know he's a virtuoso—there's a new word for you, an artist, one who's superb in his chosen work—a virtuoso cello player and he's gone because he was invited to join the Cleveland symphony, one of the country's finest orchestras, to be their leading cellist."

"Well, I did like to hear him practice—"

"And more, when you say 'creepy,' you're judging him and I don't believe God wants us to judge people, certainly not a person none of us really knew."

I remembered the Philistine conversation when he said we're all God's children and I squirmed a little and Rhoda did, too, and Mr. Gramley caught it and said, "Well, I'm making you a bit uncomfortable talking about God" and he told us he wasn't scolding us in any way, that was how he saw the world, in God's hand, and he wished everybody did but that's alright, and we were such bright girls that it was good to talk with us and after we said goodbye, I liked him just as much but I had a better idea about why he and Madeleine wouldn't, hmmm, click.

I walked by the Chapel of the Good Shepherd coming home from school next afternoon—it was Rhoda's piano day so I was alone—and I remembered what Mr. Gramley said, so I figured I might get closer to God and maybe make up a little for attending church only twice a year by going in and absorbing the hush and the stained glass light. I sat in the back and closed my eyes and thanked God for Mom and Dad, and remembered I was a sinner like everyone and asked for mercy and, since I was actually praying when you thought about it, I asked if He could get Madeleine married soon so I could have the room and when I opened my eyes, I saw Madeleine standing next to a man in the front row, and they were talking to a woman I'd seen in the Chapel sometimes.

I closed my eyes and opened them and everybody was still there and now I recognized the man, Mr. Hailey, because he'd been at our house a lot of times to pick up Madeleine, but I had sort of counted him out since he was hardly any taller than her—she—an inch or two, and there were so many others taller and more, well, *noticeable*, although he was handsome when you looked again, with sandy colored hair a little curly and this chin,

49

cleft, is what they call it, and a smile that made you smile back and he took Madeleine to the Starlight Roof where they did the Lindy Hop (I tried to imagine Mr. Gramley doing the Lindy Hop and it was funny) and Dad liked him, I remembered, because he was an engineering instructor at New York University and they had some great talks about friction and bearings and such and it all came together in my head, pow! and since I'm a family member, I should be a part of what I knew was happening right there before my eyes.

Madeleine wasn't surprised at all when I stood next to her—she knew my path home from school, it was hers before it was mine—and she slipped an arm around my shoulder and tugged me against her and introduced me to Mrs. Donaldson, who arranged events for the Chapel of the Good Shepherd, and then she said, You know Mike, of course, and he gave me that smile and said Okay if I become your brother-in-law? and I sort of lit up, because that would make me a sister-in-law, and I knew there wouldn't be anyone else in my grade who was both a sister-in-law and had her own room.

I had to wear one of those hats at the wedding, green, with a feather and bow, and a green dress which is a rotten color for me since my hair is *nondescript*, blond but not enough, and my complexion pale with some freckles and I had to listen to everyone tell me How cute you are, Janine, and Rhoda giving me those ha, ha looks—I'll get her—but that's what happens when you're a bridesmaid at your sister's wedding and you're standing in a row with the grownup bridesmaids, so Little and Precious next to them but it was over at last and we went to the Bohemian Hall for the reception and they had kielbasa and little Swedish meatballs and a thousand other foods and the band had an accordion and I was really glad then that Dad made the extra money to rent the hall and everything because Madeleine was glowing, I mean so beautiful, at the wedding and still glowing here, with the singing and dancing—polkas, waltzes, two-steps, the Big Apple, although the band kept that slow for the older people, and Rhoda's dad got a little tipsy and led us into a dance called the Hora, which we did five times and Madeleine and Mike suddenly weren't there which made everyone laugh and though I don't think serious writers should use slang, that afternoon was just *snazzy*.

So it was over and I stood in my room at bedtime with the Decca portable now on Madeleine's side, well, my other side, and my slips and socks and such spread out neatly in the drawers, no more crushing them in, and my dresses with lots of breathing room hanging in the closet and I felt free, and the other bed was there for a pajama party with Rhoda but only after a while, I wanted to enjoy a room alone first, with no noises from the other bed although I had to think back, it was kind of funny now that I'm nine, to the times when I was little and got cold in the winter or had a bad dream and I would creep into that other bed where Madeleine would call me a pest and say my feet were freezing and why don't I go bother Mom and Dad while she was making room for me and pulling me close, but that was years and years ago and I won't get *sentimental* at nine, especially when Madeleine wouldn't be far away for the next two months because she and Mike would have an apartment in Greenwich Village, near the University, while he finished his term there, and Greenwich Village was the next neighborhood south of Chelsea, ten minutes away, Rhoda and I walked there a lot, so we'd see Madeleine here or there all the time.

After that she and Mike would be in Boston because he had this terrific engineering job (fifty dollars a week, as much as Dad!) with a company that made feeder belts and things called *synchronizers* for the machine guns that go in the planes we're

The Marble King and Other Stories

sending to England for their war and Boston is five hours, twenty-eight minutes away, which I know because I stopped at the Greyhound ticket office around the corner on Eighth Avenue to get a timetable and Mom and Dad had each done the same thing and we sat in the living room with three timetables and had a big laugh although it was short.

But as I said, Boston was two months yet, and standing there in my room I didn't have to think about two months which was almost nine weeks away, sixty-two whole days, and I took one last look around at all this space and went to bed.

I woke up sometime in the darkest part of the night, the time when the streetlamps put only a little crack of light around the window shade and it was—quiet—okay, I'd get used to that but just for tonight I put on the little bedside lamp by Madeleine's—by the other—bed and got the Decca portable and played Buddy Clark singing "I'll Dance At Your Wedding" with the sound turned way down low but I guess not low enough because Mom came in and didn't say anything, just kind of smiled and put a hand on my back and lifted my arm and started dancing with me to the music, slow and dreamy, smelling like Mom in her old flannel robe—she had looked showy in her dress for the wedding and smelled perfumy and I kind of saw what Madeleine would look like when she got older—but I liked this flannel robe and Mom-smell more, and Dad came in then, too, in his undershirt and pajama bottom, carrying the Daily News—which I had remembered in the nick of time before the wedding and ran across the street to get it and I figured he wasn't sleeping that well tonight if he had been up reading—and he sat on the other bed and looked around just the way I had done before and then he looked at Mom and me dancing and said, "Well, Sugar," (what he always called Mom) and "Well, Janine, ten more years," and he slapped the paper against his knee and I figured out he meant

52

Brownstone 1940

ten more years until I got married, so there would a lot of time left for me to get the Daily News every day so it would be ready for him after supper.

If your sister stuffs your mailbox with literary magazines that depress you, and you want her to stop, there's probably a better way than this…

Endings

People say brothers and sisters fight. My sister Agnes and I were always friends. Being two years older gave her a superior tone now and then but never stopped her from playing tag or a game of Battleship or building one of my elaborate snow forts with me.

As long as she wasn't reading. Mom or Dad would have to lift a book from her hands physically some evenings to get her to the dinner table. Teachers learned to keep her in the front row to make sure she was reading her textbook, not some smuggled work of fiction.

Short stories were her special passion. When I was old enough, she'd pass them on to me, confident I would relish them as she did. It was the only time I felt I was working a little bit at our friendship.

She's a high school librarian in Baltimore now, a natural for her, and I landed a junior architect job in Providence. She still continues to feed me short stories, stuffing my mailbox with literary

The Marble King and Other Stories

magazines once she's finished with them. Do you know how many there are? How many stories?

I'm satisfied by a story now and then. It's like a clearing in a jungle. For the rest—well, I had a few vacation days saved up, so I visited Agnes last month.

"I made up a short story," I said casually after dinner. We had reached a break in the family reminiscing and were leaning back on her couch, stuffed and content.

"You? That's wonderful. Let me see it." Her eyes flicked around the room, seeking a pencil to do the necessary editing.

"It's in my head, not on paper. I could talk you through it."

"Even better. Working verbally gives us a chance to explore all the alternate themes. This is going to be fun."

"Well, the story starts in Afghanistan—"

"Starts? Where does it go?" She looked suspicious.

"Back here. Stateside."

"Sounds like there's a plot, a beginning, a middle, an end. With a resolution?"

"You know, dramatic arc." I traced it in the air. "You explained it to me."

"Eighth grade," she sighed. "Pre-history. Could you reduce it to a tragic essence plus the touch of irony every good story needs?"

"Like the one where a man murders his wife, then rents a room in Paris and broods about it, then rents a room in Vienna and broods about it and then sits on a park bench in Moscow and broods about it, while everyone who sees him thinks he's a successful writer gathering material?"

"Essence, exactly, with irony. I'm glad you liked that one."

"It could win a Pulitzer. Do they have a Best Short Essence category?"

She regarded me the way I imagine she regards a freshman who loses his library card. But then she pursed her lips and looked right through me. I remembered this from childhood. Agnes was thinking.

"You know, it could work." She thought some more. "We just might take the old formula and update it. Tell me the story and we'll find ways to channel it."

"It starts in Afghanistan," I began again. "In a tent that serves as a field chapel."

"Fine. War and religion. Things can go wrong in so many ways."

"Our hero, Danny, and his unit have one more week until they go home. The chaplain is praying for a quiet week—"

"And the soldiers get a quiet week but the chaplain steps on a mine and is killed, leaving Danny and the others wracked with guilt—"

"Well, no. They have a peaceful week, nobody's hurt and the helicopter arrives on schedule to evacuate the unit—"

"Enemy fire on the way back, down it goes, leaving the chaplain questioning his faith—"

"The helicopter brings them to the command center where they pick up discharge orders—"

"A mistake in Danny's. He has to go back into combat. He's bitter and rebellious."

"—and board a transport plane—"

"Mechanical trouble? Drunken pilot?"

"—going to the air force base in Germany where they can catch a plane for the States."

She clapped her hands. "I see it! A free night in a German city before the flight leaves. Danny wakes in the morning alone in a strange bed. There's a picture of a girl he can't remember on the nightstand—"

"The plane for home is waiting for them and they're happy to be on the way with no delay. When they land, Danny's wife, Amanda, is there to meet him, with their little boy, Danny junior. He's two years old. He's very healthy" I added, afraid she'd give the child some incurable disease. Instead, she focused on Amanda.

"She's inexplicably cold, right? Moves herself out of Danny's embrace, doesn't meet his eyes, her hair is subtly different than he remembers, a bolder shade of blonde, and her makeup, there's now more of it—"

"She's a natural strawberry redhead with curls that she hates and he loves. She wears a touch of lipstick, that's it, just like she's always done. Their greeting lasts so long, people break into applause, making them blush. Danny picks up his little boy—"

"Who doesn't know him. Who resents this stranger for hugging his Mommy. He begins to scream. The months in Afghanistan have left Danny tense and quick to burst into rage. His grip tightens on the squirming child—"

"—picks up his little boy who wraps his arms around Danny's neck, pushes his face into Danny's cheek and calls 'Daddy, Daddy, Daddy!'"

Agnes squinted to show sharp skepticism.

"Skype," I said. "Smartphones. Kids know what Daddy looks like and sounds like. And you can bet Amanda talked and talked about Daddy every day."

"Too bad," Agnes said. "Closes off some promising story lines."

"The town is dark when they arrive home—"

"Town? You want a city. Suburbs, at least. A place big enough to need a vice squad."

"Town."

"Alright. But put a meth lab nearby."

"After little Danny is asleep, Danny and Amanda sit close and thank God for bringing him back to this wonderful place. In the morning—"

"What??"

"In the morning—"

"You've forgotten the night! Post-traumatic stress for him, the strangeness of a man in bed for her. Eyes, the reader needs eyes in the bedroom, details."

"Their reunion is fine and for the reader, less," I said firmly, "is more."

Her look said Hmmph, maybe you're not so dumb.

"In the morning, his parents and her parents come over. They're all good friends, no conflict at all," I put in quickly.

"Not even a little adulterous desire? His mother and her father, say? Or status jealousy? One family's richer than the other? What do they do?"

"His family owns the local newspaper—"

"They use the presses for a pornography business on the side. Danny discovers it—"

"—and her family runs a dairy farm. Cows," I said. I made it a challenge. "Grazing in the meadow."

Agnes shrugged. There's little potential in the bovine essence.

"Danny goes to work in the family newspaper business—"

"And meets somebody who was hired while he was away. A young man, muscular yet something effeminate about him disturbs Danny—"

"—giving his father and mother some much-needed help. They had been running the business all by themselves. Danny brings some new ideas—"

"But they're too sophisticated for his small town. Nasty letters to the editor start, Amanda's friends begin cutting her off, right? Right?"

I detected a tinge of exasperation.

"—including a veteran's page, by vets, for vets. A place to exchange experiences, ask for help, offer help, let out those pent-up emotions. Danny puts it online, too—"

"Where there's ID theft and Danny is blamed. There's an official investigation, the family business is ruined, financial stress shatters the happy marriage for Danny and Amanda. Or—"

"Or?"

Exasperation had risen above the tinge level now.

"Or the idea is wildly successful, draws praise all over the country, the page is picked up by a national syndicate. That's where you're going, aren't you?"

"Actually, I was thinking global syndicate. Reuters, the Times International. Which would you prefer?"

"I would prefer that we get to the big finish." She leaned her head back into the cushions and closed one eye, then the other to indicate terminal boredom.

"Syndication makes them wealthy and after praying about it, they give most of the money to their church and to veteran's groups—"

A scornful grunt interrupted the terminal boredom.

"—just keeping enough to start a college fund for the kids."

She sat up abruptly.

"College fund? Kids?"

"Rosalie, born a year after Danny's return, followed by Sam, two years later."

Her eyes were wide open, filled with admiration.

"You sneak! You crafty little twerp!"

I hadn't heard that since the days I sank her navy playing Battleship.

"You faked me out totally," she went on. "Now I see your technique. You create all those opportunities to turn the story around, to capture the lurking tragedy, and you pass them by, teasing the reader, creating suspense step by step until it becomes screamingly unbearable. Then, at the last moment, you pull the plug. Brilliant!"

"Well, adequate at most," I said, trying to hide my bafflement.

ENDINGS

"The kids, wow. That's what you've been building to, the kids who rebel against their upbringing. Great possibilities now. Let's say Danny junior becomes an addict, Rosalie gets pregnant at fifteen, Sam joins a gang and is shot, maybe crippled for life, Danny can't handle it all and abandons them and the last thing we see is Amanda, alone in the kitchen, staring out the window, a roomful of unwashed dishes and laundry strewn around like the wreck of her marriage."

I considered the triumph and anticipation that lit her face.

We all reach these moments sooner or later, don't we?

An opinion that I drove four hundred miles to deliver suddenly didn't seem worth a walk around the block.

I clicked my mental Delete button. My actual ending—a seaside vacation where Danny and Amanda watch the kids splash in the surf and envision their bright future—was replaced by Agnes' ending. Not being a real author, I had no pangs about it.

"You did it, Sis," I confessed. "You figured it out."

She reached across and tousled my hair, taking me back twenty years.

Driving home, I thought about the girl who would come out on a shiveringly cold February day to help a little brother build a snow fort and I was pleased with the outcome of my visit. The essence, that is.

I didn't bother to point out that the ending to the story, by leaving her satisfied and happy, completely betrayed her fictional ideals.

Sooner or later, she'll realize it. I don't think she'll be too upset.

After all, it's the touch of irony every good story needs.

Live in an apartment?

You may have more family members than you suspect…

Adoption

Let me tell you about a man I'll call Edward who stands concealed by a curtain at the corner of a window in his apartment. He's watching the family on a nearby terrace.

Such moments need starting points and there are many in Edward's life. The most instructive one takes us back to fifth grade. Edward wrote a composition about urban sprawl in the Sun Belt. It was based on a local newspaper article he didn't fully grasp but the composition assignment was "Where Would I Like To Live?" and the artist's rendering of garden apartments looked inviting.

The facts were from the newspaper but the words were all Edward's.

The teacher liked the composition so much, she read it to the class after Edward sat, paralyzed, when she asked him to read it himself.

"Well, Edward, we've discovered one thing you can do," the teacher said. "You can write."

"No, he can't," came from Miranda behind him.

He had once asked Miranda to be his pretend sister. She screamed unprintable things in response. Edward had thought she was his one friend in the class.

"He stole it from a newspaper," she said

"Is that true, Edward?" the teacher asked.

Edward shook his head No, the words of explanation lodged in his throat.

"Well, then, let's move on," said the teacher.

On the bus going home, someone in the front yelled, "Well Edward, we've discovered one thing you can do." A voice from the rear answered, "You can cheat," which grew to a raucous chant joined by everyone, even first graders whose shrill voices sliced like scalpels. The chant continued most of the way to Edward's stop. When it abated, Miranda leaned over him to stage whisper, "Edward is a lying little worm." That grew into a chorus that lasted the rest of the ride. Along the way, the hidden pokes and pinches came at Edward from all sides, only harder than usual, and steadier.

Edward cut out the newspaper article. He pasted it on poster board side by side with his composition. He brought it to school the next day. The teacher said, "Thank you," and went on with the day's lessons

Long years after the composition was shredded and burned, Edward moved into a nicely furnished garden apartment. He was living in urban sprawl now and he liked it, liked having traded in a big city for a small city where you could still be just a face in the crowd. The crowd weighed less, though, and the streets were quieter. Low rise buildings displayed lawns below and unobstructed sky above. Apartment windows were wider and, in the cleaner air, the details they revealed were sharper. If you were Edward, you were happy to discover all this.

ADOPTION

You were even happier to discover terraces, a feature of the more expensive apartments in Edward's building complex, a horseshoe-shaped affair that found Edward on the second floor at the curve of the horseshoe. That placed his windows to the side of a higher priced apartment and its terrace. There were no terraces on the ground floor and the third floor terrace belonged to an elderly couple who sat without sound or motion. When the neighboring family was on their terrace, there were no other voices to interfere. He had never had such a vantage point.

Edward was now grateful to the officials responsible for his move. It was so hard to bond with a family in the rabbit warrens of the city. It could take months. Here, it required only a few days, starting with the sight of a doll left in a chair on the terrace. Edward waited. Before his watch ticked off an hour, a girl, about eight years old, came out to claim the doll. A good start.

The next day revealed father, mother and little brother. All Edward needed after that was a carefully tuned ear to conversations on the terrace, a peek at the names on the mailboxes downstairs, a quick search through the business pages of the phone book, and he was settled in. No family ever made it easier to join.

The little girl—her name was Gloria—captivated Edward quickly. Blond pigtails, harlequin spectacles, a pensive air and a habit of arguing with herself were endearing enough, but the bug rescue sealed it for him. She appeared on the terrace one afternoon with something carefully enclosed in one hand. At the rail, she took a mighty breath and blew away a ladybug, calling, "Now stay out here. In the house, you could get squished." She shook her head like an anxious mother.

Minus the words and the headshake, Edward did the same thing with any friendly insect that wandered inside. Now I realize these deliverances are everyday events—I've gently evicted many a cricket myself—but this is Edward we're talking about. By this

65

point you probably understand how little mercy he had seen in his life. He made a V for Victory sign at Gloria's back as she went inside. They were linked by something essential.

Incidentally, please reject any unpleasant suspicions about Edward's feelings. He had no perverted appetites for children. His affection for Gloria was that of a favorite uncle, which is how he saw himself, having aged beyond the brother and cousin stages of previous families. Looking in a mirror, Edward could be realistic.

He took this family role seriously, trying to keep himself close, in his way, to Rob, Gloria's dad; Pamela, her mom, and Mikey, her little brother, nine months old. Fond looks were all he could manage in that case since baby talk was a blank page in Edward's memory.

Another discovery for Edward was the school bus. It began its route on the curved street below, a stroke of luck that found him at the window every morning, waiting with Gloria. He filled the time with little waves and smiles, while inspecting the kids around her. They were talking, yawning, jostling, laughing, all without a visible bully among them. Not one. When Gloria boarded the bus, he was confident she would continue chattering happily all the way to school. For Edward, could there be a better start to the day?

Walks by the school playground were another way he connected. He could always spot Gloria in the recess crowd. He used to stop and quietly wave a few fingers at her. Our secret, he would tell himself. He gave that up following an incident with a sheriff's deputy. The little computers they keep in patrol cars these days turned out to be a blessing. The deputy found out in a moment that Edward didn't have so much as a jay-walking ticket. Still, he just kept moving after that, ending up at a nearby

Chinese restaurant. "Very good menu," he told the hostess each day. "No place like this in my neighborhood."

Connecting with Rob was more difficult. Gloria went to school and she spared ladybugs, mutual experiences that made her the natural channel to the family. Rob was a lawyer. The phone book had revealed he handled things like wills and real estate and business contracts, matters that Edward grasped only in the vague way most of us do.

Rob's office was in a building downtown where people were always milling about. Nobody noticed or cared if Edward lingered outside with the smokers. He would hold an unlit cigarette in his hand like a hall pass, picturing Rob in his office with a young couple. They were about to buy their first home and were a little jittery about the new responsibilities. Rob explained deeds and mortgages and such so cheerfully, they relaxed and let slip a little secret: a baby was on the way. Rob congratulated them and turned the photos on his desk so they could see his own family. It was a satisfying scene, every time.

He worked up the courage to walk past the office itself one day. Rob usually left for lunch at 12:30, and Edward would nod at him, then add a little personal smile. Rob was always talking to a client, or one of the other lawyers as they eased through the crowd, so he didn't notice, which was quite alright. Edward had done his part.

When he saw Rob leave this particular day, he entered the building carrying a large manila envelope. The few people still inside were heading for the exits, lunch obviously on their minds. He went up the stairs to an empty hallway and found Rob's office. He studied the gold script: Robert Carlton, Attorney, as understated and elegant as he expected.

He walked up and down the hallway several times, slowing to observe Rob's office at each pass, until voices sounded in the stairwell. Prominently displaying the envelope, he went back down to the street and outside, looking straight ahead in a businesslike manner. A little thrill overtook him; he had done something daring, like a spy mission. What if he had been approached? Asked what was in the envelope? Well, the risk was worth it. The connection to Rob was that much stronger now.

He was thankful for the small supermarket in town. It gave him the chance to spend some time with Pamela. When she left the apartment house with Mikey in the stroller, he would get his shopping bag and leave, too. If they didn't share the same streets—Edward took a different route, knowing from experience about demented old ladies peering through the blinds, ready to see a stalker in every passerby—if they didn't share the same streets, they did share the same sunshine and the same aisles in the supermarket, just a few minutes apart.

He performed the smoker routine a few times outside the market where he could nod in her direction as she talked to her friends or fussed over Mikey and where he could take an inventory of what was in the cart. Jimmy Dean sausage was not his breakfast favorite, and he preferred Sprite to Pepsi, but he always adapted to the rest of the family's tastes. It was no sacrifice, really.

The family went to church regularly, so Sunday morning for Edward meant dressing with extra care. Polished shoes, ironed white shirt, dark suit, a tastefully matched tie and he was ready. He let them know with a little salute as they left. He had kept his Bible for Young Readers all these years, pages still crisp. He held it on his lap and closed his eyes, bringing back the music and the sermons, words not mattering, riding the minister's voice like a roller coaster, just as in childhood. He shared a private smile with everybody when they returned, certain they had all done the same thing.

The family prayed a lot, too. On the terrace every twilight, while Mikey slept in a playpen, Rob and Pamela and Gloria joined hands and bowed their heads, taking turns. Edward bowed his head, too, and played the Father of God game. He praised Him for those things that deserved praise while pointing out the areas where correction was needed in a calm and straightforward manner.

And now it's time to take a deep breath. The troublesome part is here. Well, more than just troublesome. I've been painting the good days, the days when every member of the family was wonderfully in place for Edward, truly the most peaceful days he had known since his mom died. Disrupting them is hard.

For the last five days, he's been at the window almost every minute trying to keep a close watch on Marilyn. She arrived Monday in a clattering yellow Jeep Wrangler. He heard enough conversation to learn her name, to learn that she's Pamela's cousin, that she's a prodigy—high school at twelve, two college degrees at eighteen—and now she's writing a PHD thesis that will keep her in the guest room for several months.

The simple family structure was overturned. To his credit, Edward tried. He told himself over and over: this is not directed at you, not this time. And in fact, it was different from previous assaults, where prying neighbors or bad-tempered family members were the invaders.

So why didn't she spend the whole day inside writing? A thesis takes a long time; he had heard her complain about it herself. But now when the bus returned, instead of Pamela waiting, there was Marilyn, in her faded jeans, oversize man's shirt, scuffed sneakers, those little steel-rimmed glasses—what an amateurish touch, he said to himself—that endless smile, the whole university girl charade.

They sat on the terrace each afternoon sharing Gloria's after-school milk and cookies and then they played on the lawn, batting a badminton bird or a croquet ball. Sometimes, they took little Mikey for a walk in his stroller. That moved them out of sight for a while. He didn't know which was more frustrating, watching them or being unable to watch them. When they returned, they went back to the terrace to read books and play games, whooping and laughing, or at times sitting with heads together, whispering like class mates. Marilyn never glanced Edward's way, although once when they played Go Fish, he saw her shoulders shake as she shifted her chair in front of Gloria, blocking her from any outside view. It wasn't laughter, he insisted. It wasn't deliberate. She hadn't seen him, didn't know he was around.

After prayer that night, Marilyn and Rob sat talking on the terrace while Pamela took the kids inside. Marilyn had a writing tablet in her lap, jotting words down now and then by the terrace lamp. Edward supposed she was claiming her PHD had something to do with the law and she needed Rob as a source.

Except what part of her thesis called for the little trick with her hair? She wore it tied in a bun, but as Rob was talking and looking at her, she shook it free to stream down her back, like a scene from a bad movie romance. And the next moment, her eyes turned Edward's way. With the light soft and the street dark, was she darting a glance of triumph that Rob would never notice? Edward replayed the sight again and again, peering inward to examine it. Yes, he finally concluded, it was possible. It was possible.

He discarded any suspicion that Pamela was trying to be a home wrecker. Rob and Pamela still looked at each other like teenagers with a crush. The marriage was invulnerable and Marilyn was smart enough to see that. She was also smart enough to know that even the most faithful of men can be won over by a little flirtation. Rob is a friend now, if he wasn't before.

The next morning, Edward was at the window, ready for the cheerful school bus scene that began his day. When Gloria came out, carrying her books, he started to wave, until he noticed Marilyn following her. They went to the parking area, not the bus stop. With a look at the clear sky, they wrestled the canvas top off the jeep. Gloria hollered, "You rule!" at the colorful open air vehicle.

Edward lay down with a warm compress, trying to rid his mind of the sight of Marilyn and Gloria driving off, the jeep's vanity license plate a final insult: SMARTERNU.

When Pamela and Mikey went into town later, he followed them all the way to the market, staying a mere half a block behind. Desperate, yes, he admitted it. If any demented old ladies were watching through their blinds, he just didn't care. He had to have some contact, some reassurance of the family link. He even walked down the aisles after Pamela, filling his cart with the same items she bought. If the cashier wondered why someone like him wanted Gerber's mashed peas, it was her problem.

In the afternoon, he walked to school at dismissal hour. He didn't keep moving this time. He stood and watched. The sheriff's deputies had to be risked. If Marilyn was going to be there, he couldn't simply leave the field, vanquished. At the least, he had to know about it.

"There she is," he said happily, seeing Gloria emerge and head for the bus line. Then the jeep pulled up. Library books tumbled around in the rear seat, no doubt Marilyn's cover story for being in town. Edward whipped a tissue from his pocket, pretending a sneeze to hide his anger. Just to make the scene a little more galling, all the kids began cheering when Gloria bounded into the passenger seat. She pumped her fists in the air in glee. Edward was too frustrated even to wave as the vehicle rattled down the street.

That evening, Edward rallied a little. Time on the terrace had passed smoothly with everybody in a circle, praying, talking quietly and although Gloria and Marilyn were sitting close, Marilyn's attention had been focused on little Mikey, holding him as he slept, rocking him and playing with his hair. When everyone was inside and the lights turned on, he called his regular "Goodnight all" to the lowered bedroom shades.

Normally he would head for bed himself at that point but there was an odd shadow through the gauzy drapes of the living room. No, *shadows*. Two of them, distorted by the room lights, surreally blossoming and shrinking. A tall shadow, bending to and fro like a birch. A smaller one, lunging, trying to imitate the other. A dance lesson, the stuff he guessed they did at college recitals, almost hypnotic here. He watched the swallow-like swoops, the backward bends, the suddenly upraised arms, the slow twirls, first the tall shadow, then the small shadow, the small one growing steadily surer until the two finally flowed in unbroken harmony, swooping, bending, twirling, totally merged.

The shadows disappeared, the lights went out. The final image stayed, imprinted in Edward's vision. He sat staring at the dark windows. Marilyn's spell was complete; she had drawn Gloria to herself in a matter of days. Where would she take it from here? If she's one of those who gain pleasure from dominating others, there's only one direction: tighter and tighter control.

Is it conceivable Rob or Pamela were blind to the potential problem? It might be. Rob's occupied with work, Pamela with Mikey, Marilyn's a familiar and favorite cousin, surely looking innocent when they're all together—the forest and the trees; it took somebody outside to observe it. And Gloria's at such an impressionable age. Learning to be in thrall to someone could subtly warp her for life. The possibility was alarming and he saw no way to guard against it.

He was still staring when the sun came up, the lights went on, and Gloria and Marilyn went off again in the jeep. He paced back and forth, unable to repel the image of the carnival-like ride, the noisy arrival at school. He stopped pacing, started to ponder something. School. Where there was a psychologist on call or a social worker trained to spot hidden symptoms. A phone call? No, talking made him nervous and people wanted simplicity and certainty on the phone. A letter then, to the principal. Edward could handle that discreetly. After all, one thing you can do, Edward, you can write.

His fifth draft seemed acceptable. He kept a neutral tone, framing everything in questions: what can the school do about stealthy emotional manipulation? Suppose it's by a trusted relative? Is there regular screening of students? Are teachers alert to the signs? Are parents notified immediately? Edward pointed out that he was not trained, that this was a gray area where hard evidence was not easy to gather, so he was simply raising the issues. Satisfied with this diplomatic handling, he took it to the mail box.

The principal's secretary scanned the letter, the forty-first piece of mail she had opened that morning. She stapled a Suspected Abuse form to it, sent it on to Child Protective Services and continued to the forty-second piece of mail.

They refused to bring charges.

The fact made sense slowly to Edward, his mind still swirling with the absurdity of it all. He was trying to protect them. Now he was the accused. Through the warped lens of Child Protective Services, the child was not harmed in any way. Her cousin's actions were normal and affectionate. The family believed it.

The Services people had brought the sheriff along. An informal meeting, they said. When is a badge ever informal? The sheriff held a notebook open like a menu. Did the family want to press charges: slander, harassment, voyeurism, invasion of privacy?

Edward looked at them for the first time. His eyes had caromed away before, as if avoiding the noonday sun. They were seated around a long conference table, all but Gloria, whose voice could be heard from the reception room where she waited with a Child Services aide. Edward surveyed the conference room for another exit when this was over, found none.

"No charges, no legal action," Rob said.

The sheriff looked doubtful. "How about you, Mrs. Carlton?" Pamela had been staring at the table. She glanced at Edward now and he saw the contradiction in her face. The brow drawn tightly in fury, the lioness and her cub, yes, but also the eyes inspecting him, trying to see a jackal, not finding one. I'm prey, not predator, please, Edward thought.

All she said to the sheriff was, "I agree with my husband."

"You, Miss?" the sheriff asked Marilyn. "You were the target of the accusation."

"No charges," she said, regarding Edward with no anger visible, only open curiosity, as if he might be the subject of a term paper. He suppressed an irrational urge to giggle.

"Suppose he does this again?" the sheriff persisted. "Menaces another family?"

"A menace?" Rob said before Marilyn could answer. "I've checked his record. I'm sure you have, too."

"Alright, he's clean, never a charge of any kind. But if he's not a menace, he's certainly a nuisance."

"Each and every one of us is a nuisance, Sheriff, in one way or another." Rob was laughing as he said it. And Rob was not laughing as he said it. Lawyers must learn how to do that, Edward decided, impressed.

"Well, at least he will have to move. We've spoken to the building management. They're not as forgiving as you are." There was a little barb to it.

"It's a proper decision for a building manager." Rob was mild now. "And not pressing charges is different than forgiving. For that, we'll call on the Lord to lead us and pull us together." He nodded toward Pamela, who was expressionless, and Marilyn, who regarded Edward steadily now, her head tilted, eyes narrowed in deep thought.

The sheriff shrugged and said, "It's your call, Counselor." He faced Edward for a moment, calculating something. "Your call," he repeated to Rob and closed the notebook.

"No," said Marilyn suddenly. "He won't do it again." She called to the sheriff at the door, "This was the last time." The sheriff shook his head and walked out.

Edward breathed again, thinking of "just a nuisance" and the deliberate way Rob had softened the sting for him. He tried to recall another time when somebody actually heard what was being said, considered it from the nuisance's point of view—and Marilyn? Where had her pronouncement come from? What sort of deception was at work?

By waiting when the others left, Edward managed to avoid Gloria in the reception room but in the parking lot she was looking back at him, Pamela gripping her hand, tugging her along, Gloria fighting the grip, slowing them.

"Do you ever pray about things?" she yelled.

Pamela slipped her arms around Gloria's waist to pick her up. Edward heard scattered words of Gloria's protest. "I was only… God's children…you always tell me…" Rob whispered something to Pamela and she released Gloria.

75

Edward finally forced some sound through his parched throat. "I don't pray about things. I think about things." He meant it to be light, whimsical, as one talks to a child. Having to yell made it come out cracked and harsh. The idea that he might have offended Gloria now was painful.

"That's really cool," she answered, meaning it. "You can think about praying."

The following morning, he took a bus into the next county, some twenty minutes away, and found a suitable place. The furniture was sparse and shabby but he paid little attention to that, and little to the houses and windows close by, glancing at them out of habit alone, not even attracted by a picture window opposite with a clear line of sight.

He returned and started packing, keeping away from the view of the terrace. Experience had shown him that much. No tearful farewells. They took too much out of you.

Better to look ahead, not back. It's done.

Of course, there was the matter of praying. He owed that to Gloria. She had been so totally trusting. Dim memories of Sunday School came back, memories of praying as hard as he could that he would be ignored. This time, with a different purpose, prayer might have a better chance.

And Rob was owed gratitude. No charges. Firm with the sheriff about it.

Should he write to the family? As always, he could explain things best on paper, try to make Pamela understand. They might reply—Rob out of politeness, certainly—perhaps with Pamela joining if Edward explained well.

He let his mind roam to letters back and forth, enough so an invitation might come. No, unthinkable. Well, think about it any-

ADOPTION

way. A Christian family, aren't they called on to reach out? An invitation. Edward's fingers twitched as if opening it and a wispy image came of a Sunday afternoon grill on the terrace. He'd memorize the right things to say, like I can only stay a short while. Even if he sat mute and listened they just might understand. Only a twenty minute bus ride. Another lemonade, Edward? I have the suit and tie for church, should it ever go that far —

How long had the doorbell been chiming?

The sheriff was there, with a man he introduced as the county attorney.

"We've been doing some checking up," the attorney said. He was quick and blunt, a man in charge of things. "Your previous addresses, your bank records, items like that. Did you find a new apartment?"

Edward nodded.

"Where?"

Edward told him.

"We'll give you a month there. Use that month to find a place across the state line. No more of these short distance moves. If you don't agree, we'll go to court, have you declared incompetent, attach the income from your mother's insurance and find a supervised home for you to live in."

The nearest state line was two hundred miles away.

"I figure you'll agree," put in the sheriff. "It's the smarter choice. And something you should keep in mind: we'll tell the law enforcement people wherever you go to drop in now and then, make sure you're okay."

He understood. A police visit will make the neighbors suspicious, watchful. No more new families, Edward. He tried to find pain in that but it was elusive, like a sail slipping over the horizon.

Two trips would do it, he decided, looking over his suitcases and packages. He made the first in the afternoon, feeling eyes on him as he left. The whole building would know of the episode, of course. He returned after sunset, grateful to find TV lights flickering behind windows and no curious neighbors in his path.

A misty twilight settled in and Edward went to the window, breaking his rule. He needed a farewell now. He left all the lights off, even the inside hallway bulb he usually kept burning, so there would be no sign that he was home. The family was assembling for evening prayers. Little Mikey dozed in his playpen, one small hand reaching out, touching the face of Gloria's doll. Yes, she would give him a favorite plaything, with a motherly caution to "Take good care of her." He smiled at Gloria, facing him on the terrace, a white flower barrette in her hair. He automatically checked Marilyn's hair for one that matched. The hairpins that held the bun glinted. There was nothing else.

They moved close and prayers began. He recognized for the first time how important the serenity of this hour had become for him. Seeing Gloria off to school in the morning, prayer on the terrace in the evening. They were cupped hands, enclosing his day.

The mist became a light rain, turning the air fresh and cool, not disturbing the bowed heads, the murmuring voices, the peace that Edward was savoring. *Now*, only *now*, he insisted as thoughts of tomorrow intruded.

When the others went inside, hurrying against the rain, Marilyn walked slowly to the railing. Wondering, Edward watched her turn her head from side to side, arching her neck, stretching it. Then she did the hair trick. It flowed down her back and she began to dance. What in the world is she trying to prove? Those bends and swoops again, arms stretched up, slow twirls—for whose benefit? She couldn't know he was there. He was well concealed and there was little light left. She wasn't looking in his direction, anyway. She was looking up, breaking into different movements, crazy rag-doll jumping now, arms shaking, flopping, knees bent in, knees bent out, and she stopped, standing at the rail again, head way back, moving her face in the raindrops, tongue out now, catching them, grinning, just enough light left for Edward to see the silly smile...

She's a kid!

Look at her.

How old can she be? Eighteen? Nineteen? A PHD candidate, yes, but one who catches raindrops and drives a yellow SMART-ERNU jeep, a toy with a motor. One who probably missed a lot of childhood being a prodigy. A schoolgirl at heart. With a malevolent side? Can you dance in the rain like a rag doll one minute and be treacherous the next? Or harbor some malicious purpose in telling the sheriff, "He won't do this again," actually a childish proclamation when you think about it?

While Edward weighed all this, Gloria came out to stand at the rail and imitate Marilyn until Pamela put her head out and yelled, "The two of you! You're soaked! Get inside!" Hunching their shoulders, pantomiming guilty children, giggling, they tiptoed through the door.

Back in the new apartment, Edward sat motionless by the window, stirring only when the first beams of daylight fell across him. He had no memory of falling asleep. There was a dream, though, where Rob was making a speech in a stadium filled with terraces while the sheriff danced back and forth behind him.

His watch read five o'clock. Four hours until Rob arrived at the office.

Enough time to compose a letter and mail it. No, deliver it.

He made an outline. The explanations, an apology to Marilyn—she would be sympathetic, maybe help to persuade Pamela—and then the legal questions: can they deport me to another state? Have me declared incompetent ? I pay the rent, file tax returns,

The Marble King and Other Stories

balance my bank accounts, all of that. Can they really attach my income without cause? Arrange to have me harassed wherever I go? No, they couldn't. They couldn't. Rob would reassure him.

Would Rob represent him if it actually went to court?

He crossed that one out, re-entered it, crossed it out, walked around the apartment, then re-entered it and underlined it. Rob had defended him in front of the sheriff. I have nobody else. Rob would understand.

Edward arrived fifteen minutes before nine, admired again the neat gold script on the door, the way it inspired confidence, and placed the envelope right above it. He took the roll of tape from his pocket and affixed the envelope with a strip at each corner. He tapped it to make certain it was secure, caught the next bus back to his new home and sat by the phone.

This story is fiction.
There are no parking enforcers in New York City.
There is no Mr. Kimmelman.
There is no executive committee.
There is no Staten Island.

Meter Maid

Katie Dutton made crucial decisions twice about parking violations on her beat. The first led to headlines and a Supreme Court case.

The second was more important.

This needs explaining, of course, and the best place to start is Eighth Avenue one January morning where a street preacher named Arlen Gross gazed east at Forty-fourth Street, satisfied. He had just placed a tract called 'The Servant Heart' under the wiper of every parked car. Other than setting up a flag, holding a Bible and preaching—which he was about to do, despite snowflakes arriving—this is the way God's word is transmitted in New York City by its pavement evangelists.

"Like a West Point review," said Katie, turning from the avenue for her second tour of Forty-fourth. She waved up the street at the field of precisely placed, uniformly upright tracts adorning the windshields.

"I was obeying Galatians 6:4," Arlen responded, looking a challenge at her.

"Pay close attention to your work, for then you will have the satisfaction of a job well done," she recited. "That's an easy one, Arlen."

"Tomorrow, look out," he answered. "I may go to Leviticus."

She threw up her hands in mock surrender and resumed her beat, keeping a steady pace until she spotted the dented green Plymouth still parked near the Shubert building, inviting a citation. She fingered the ticket writer at her belt but slowed, drifted across the street to the Broadhurst and pretended to read the theatre's posters, thinking she'd give a little extra time to the Plymouth's owner.

She had seen him enter the building without a coat, only a vest, not even a hat, evidently someone who didn't check weather forecasts. Her father had been that way, rest in peace. This fellow was about the age her father would be and, like him he was small and slightly balding. Well, millions of men look like that she reminded herself when she finished the last poster. Pay close attention to your work.

She printed out the ticket and slipped it under the wiper, where it pushed 'The Servant Heart' sideways. She straightened up the tract and started to close her book.

"Hey, lady, come on!" The owner had emerged from the building.

Just a minute earlier, she thought.

"I'm sorry, sir. We have a job to do."

She walked on, following instructions to avoid confrontations.

Pausing to mark a Chevy pickup a few cars down, she looked over to see the man cram the citation into a trousers pocket, read the cover of the tract, crumple it and throw it on the ground. Halfway into his car, he paused, stepped out and looked the street over. He bent and retrieved the tract. Shaking snowflakes from it, he smoothed it with care, smiled and slipped it into his shirt pocket.

There was some doubt in Katie's mind that the smile was for her—it had a distant quality—but she smiled back. Obviously, he was happy with the tract. She'd have to tell Arlen. Every little crumb of encouragement counted.

Twenty-five years as a theatrical attorney, Leonard Swain thought, twenty-five years, and I'm kept waiting like a beverage salesman. And the work they give, writing some road company contract. A week's income and they'll make me wait two months to see the check. His frame of mind was so bleak he didn't even notice the snow. The parking ticket he greeted with a shrug; he knew the person to call, and this, what, a Jesus tract? These people just don't know where to stop. Here, let them give me a littering ticket, too.

Oh, wait.

Suppose…

He picked it out of the snow.

Yes, why not?

After all, he actually eye-witnessed her putting it under the wiper.

Leonard nearly broke the door down rushing into his apartment. He greeted his wife with, "I don't want to hear about your dental work or the kid's college payment." He tore into the spare bedroom where he kept his shelf of tattered law books.

Two days later, in the locker room at the end of her shift, Katie ignored the crackle of the loudspeaker coming to life. An employee dinner, a retirement party, discount theatre tickets—with an ill and aging mother to care for, there was no social calendar for her.

The Marble King and Other Stories

She could handle it, the workdays being as satisfactory as they were. In a diary she had kept since junior high, entered in gold ink were words assembled from poems by Walt Whitman: *"Thou portal, thou arena...thou like the parti-colored world itself, like infinite, teeming, mocking life...Give me such shows... Give me the streets of Manhattan!"* She had discovered the lines in a seventh grade English class and felt herself an actress walking home that afternoon, a member of the cast, conscious for the first time that the 'parti-colored world' wouldn't look the same without her. Significant now, she took to strolling midtown, from the six-lane avenues of neon facades and dollar shops and determined traffic to the narrow embrace of side streets with their brownstones and theatres and tiny restaurants down a few enticing steps. She cheerfully observed—in that guarded Manhattan way—the faces around her, her fellow cast members in their never ending variety, glum, grinning, wide eyed, mesmerized, meditative, furtive, triumphant...give me such shows! When the time came for a job, she knew just where to apply.

The crackling came through to her, and the insistent voice.

Kathryn Dutton to the executive conference room, Kathryn Dutton to the executive conference room.

She was up the stairs and halfway there when the enormity of it struck her. Nobody called a mere parking enforcement officer to the executive conference room. Even her supervisor and her supervisor's supervisor never went there. It was for the very top level, directors, deputy directors, visiting congressmen and such.

Bernie Smith was half a flight behind her. He had been clocking out, thinking once again that the union was just too doggone big. A shop steward in one small local could never make a name for himself when the parent union was one of those coast-to-coast conglomerates: TV and phone technicians, factory workers, flight attendants, heavy equipment operators, public health people, educators, on and on, all gathered into an alliance great for a national issue but where did it leave Bernie Smith and his little crew of New York parking enforcers? It was a real long shot that something worthwhile was brewing here, just that the loudspeaker summons made his nerve endings tingle. Katie Dutton? That lamb? Why would the top brass call her?

"Hey, Katie, wait! I'm going with you."

Katie's thankful look when he reached her made Bernie satisfied he had come. Shop stewards protect the flock.

He ushered her through the double doors as though the conference room belonged to him. A blur of solemn, male middle aged faces around a long table greeted them. Mr. Kimmelman, the executive director himself, stood at the end of the table.

He looked at Bernie. "Aren't you the shop steward?" He made it sound like a felony. "This is not a union matter."

Bernie did some lightning-like counting. His nerve-endings tingled again. Something big *was* simmering.

"I see twelve management representatives at this table," Bernie responded. "The executive director, the deputy directors, staff directors, people with briefcases—lawyers, if I'm not mistaken." He held Katie's arm. "Here I see one union member. One. Do you expect her shop steward to leave her alone and defenseless?"

"What I expect from the union," Mr. Kimmelman began, then stopped at a warning hand from one of the briefcase men. He picked a sheet of paper from the table and turned to Katie.

"Ms. Dutton, did you put a religious tract on the window of a green, 1994 Plymouth, license NY3AR4253 on Monday morning at three minutes after ten?"

"What nonsense," Bernie said. "Of course, she didn't."

The Marble King and Other Stories

"I only straightened it up," she said.

"Straightened it up?" asked Mr. Kimmelman.

"Only straightened it up," Bernie corrected firmly, although his feet shifted a little.

"The citation I put on the windshield knocked it sideways," Katie explained, "so I put it back, upright, you know." She moved her hands up and down to indicate vertical to Mr. Kimmelman, then repeated it for the briefcase men.

"And the religious tracts on all the other cars on the street?"

"They were already upright."

"Because you placed them that way?"

"Oh, no. Arlen Gross placed them that way."

Mr. Kimmelman motioned to one of the briefcase men, who handed him a stack of papers in a blue cover. Brass clips held it together. Mr. Kimmelman shook it at her. "Do you know what this is?"

A bewildered Katie peered at the papers.

"A lawsuit! A lawsuit for five million dollars against the city of New York for trying to establish a religion, for promoting a particular religion, thereby violating this gentleman's rights under the First Amendment to the Constitution plus twenty-three Federal, state and city laws, statutes and codes." He tapped the papers. "This gentleman says he witnessed you placing the tracts. So who's Arlen Gross? Can he refute this witness?"

"Yes, yes," Katie almost yelled. "He's the evangelist who preaches on Eighth Avenue. I'll go—"

"This is all very simple then," cut in Bernie, the conversation having gone on long enough without him. "Mr. Gross will confess his part and put an end to this. We'll be in touch. Come along, Kathryn."

"No, I won't," Arlen explained for the third time to a disbelieving Katie. He was patient and serious. "People won't care about a street preacher placing tracts. Happens every day. But a city employee, well, that's headline news. 'The Servant Heart' will be mentioned, even shown, on all the channels, the Internet, You Tube. Just imagine the attention it will get."

"Just imagine the attention I will get!"

"And more," Arlen went on, "the whole issue of religious freedom will be debated. People will have to question whether a person's job should keep her from expressing her faith."

"A government employee on duty? Arlen, that question was settled long ago."

"We'll unsettle it."

"Arlen, please, I will lose my job."

He looked triumphantly at her. "Katie, most martyrs lose their lives."

Katie bit her lip in frustration. Then she thought of martyrs and their saintliness. This should do it. "Christians are bound to be truthful, Arlen. You know that and you're asking me to lie."

"Not at all. You're going to say you didn't place the tracts, which is the truth. It's no fault of yours if people don't believe you."

It was Katie's turn to look triumphant. "Then you'll have to lie, saying you didn't do it. Are you ready to do that? You know you're not."

Arlen smiled benignly.

"I won't be here."

Katie sat at a small steel desk in a seven by eight foot cubicle, surrounded by scores of similar cubicles, in a room the size of a school cafeteria, answering phone calls from the owners of ticketed or towed-away vehicles. She had learned to hold the phone at a distance.

Bernie reached over the waist high partition to bestow an encouraging pat on the shoulder.

"Since January, Bernie," Katie moaned. She waved at the rows of cubicles. "I appreciate that you visit every day, but it's six months now."

"We've been through this, kid. The reporters and the TV crews would be thick as flies again if you went back. You couldn't do your job."

"Well, what about Arlen? Can't anybody find him? He'll be preaching wherever he is. He couldn't stop himself."

"The union has detective agencies working, every city. Doing our best, but it's not easy. Preachers are cagey. Look, I gotta run. You hang on, kid. Remember, our case is on the docket. We'll be in court next month."

"Next month," she repeated with a heavy sigh.

———————————————

The city offered a million to settle out of court but Leonard Swain sneered and turned it over to one of his newly hired paralegals to turn down. "Be curt," he instructed. "This is a matter of principle."

He was famous now and fame brings business to a lawyer, especially one willing to tackle city hall. Crusading Leonard Swain, as the media instantly labeled him, no longer visited theatre owners; they came to him. So did businesses from all five boroughs convinced their rights were being trampled by city zoning laws, safety codes, environmental standards and parking regulations. More, Leonard's reception area was packed with workers refused a city job, fired from a city job, injured on a city job or harassed on a city job. Leonard was amazed at the number of enemies a metropolis could generate, although not too amazed to demand a retainer in advance.

Then there was the Swain Foundation for Civic Freedom, set up last week with his wife—her smile agleam with new dental work—as principal officer. His son, about to graduate college, all paid for, was penciled in as the other principal. Contributions already topped three hundred thousand dollars.

"Thank you, Ms. Kathryn Dutton," Leonard murmured, leaning back, admiring the view of Park Avenue from his new office. What a bountiful six months that parking ticket had brought! The ticket and Leonard Swain's quick thinking, of course.

"How many are there?" Katie asked in frustration. "City Court, State Supreme Court, Appelate Court, Federal District Court, Federal Appeals Court, the real Supreme Court—"

"And that's where we are, finally," Bernie exulted. "Washington, D.C. Arguments next week. Never been a case on such a fast track."

"Fast track? Fast track?" Her voice went up like a siren in the crowded Burger King. "A year and a half of—of—*that!*" She stood and pointed across the street at the parking enforcement office.

"Shh, shh," Bernie cautioned, although other lunchtime diners paid no attention.

Katie sat down. "Everyone around here gets up and screams at least once a day. Next week for sure?"

"For sure, and you make history. Freedom of religion, freedom of speech, pillars of the Constitution re-examined, all thanks to Katie Dutton. Plus property rights and search and seizure. Swain is challenging the whole enforcement thing, from sticking a ticket on private property to towing it away."

The Marble King and Other Stories

"And after the arguments, how long until a verdict?"

"A case this complicated? Probably take until the end of the term, a few months." He waved a half-eaten French fry at her. "A little more patience. Then history, Katie, history to be made."

The reappearance of Arlen Gross, stouter by twenty pounds and tanned by the New Mexico sun, put a brake on the making of history.

"I would like to give you a national scoop," he announced solemnly to the editor of the weekly West Arroyo City Tribune, circulation 1,300, in the publication's office over the West Arroyo City Bakery.

"You're the new preacher with a church in his trailer, right? Pastor Timothy you call yourself. You got a divine tip about the Second Coming?"

"Timothy's my middle name. Arlen Timothy Gross. Here." He handed over a newspaper clipping.

The editor glanced, glanced again, studied Arlen and said, "I'll be damned. Excuse me, Reverend, figure of speech." He grabbed for the phone.

That evening, Arlen held a copy of 'The Servant Heart' before an array of TV cameras. "The most famous tract ever published," he proclaimed. "An entire nation has read it, has seen the Word. My mission is done, the Lord's purpose is accomplished." He went on to confess that he was the one who placed the tracts on the windshields. His friend, Katie Dutton, was innocent, totally, and he wanted to save her any more hardship now that the Supreme Court was ready to consider the case. "With God's guidance, we'll have a new light shining on the matter of state interference with the rights of believers."

Even a street smart preacher can be naïve at times.

METER MAID

A collective sigh of relief emanated from the Supreme Court when Arlen finished. Casebooks on the intricacies of Constitutional law were slapped shut, bottles of aspirin and Visine went back into their desk drawers, hidden decanters of Scotch came out and on the following day, the Chief Justice announced the case was now moot. Its basic premise—a government employee on duty promoting a religion—had no basis in fact and so no further action was needed. All nine justices recommended that lower courts vacate their decisions. The slate was clean.

Katie finished her sandwich, trying to get used to the solitude of the waterfront in October. Kids in school, swimming season over, just some lunchtime softball players in the park behind her, their cries faint, mostly drowned out by the squawks of gulls swooping above or—the daring ones—landing to perform their aggressive little parade steps around her bench.

"Is it me or the tuna?" Katie asked, flicking a left-over shred toward the nearest parader. The bird pounced and flew off with it. "Yeah, I thought so," Katie said, following the dipping, soaring flight. "You fly better than a pigeon," she called out, "but I like pigeons more, Manhattan pigeons, dirty and dumb. You're too clean."

She spent a few more minutes watching the tug and barge and ferry traffic of the deepwater bay that separates Staten Island from the rest of the city. The Verazzano bridge to Brooklyn soared high and inaccessible in the distance. Brooklyn, she thought, a real borough, linked to Manhattan: a subway ride and you're there, Forty-fourth Street, the theatres, the walkers, the talkers, the horns…

Katie smoothed her uniform skirt and headed back toward the boulevard. "Staten Island will be much more relaxing," Mr.

93

Kimmelman had said. Bernie agreed. "Not an exile, kid, a nice change of pace. Families shopping, small businesses, slow traffic, no Manhattan taxis"—he pantomimed jumping back in terror—"and you'll be outside, no more telephone cubicle, right?"

And none of the attention she'd invite if she went back to Manhattan streets. She understood.

The sea air is good for us, her mother had told her. The new apartment over a suburban family's garage was small but neat, easy for Katie to clean, and the family was friendly, the children fun. Grandma, they called her mother, to her delight. There was even a yard where they could enjoy a sunny day.

All in all, Katie insisted to herself, things had turned out well for her, as they certainly had for everyone else.

Arlen Gross now pastored Servant Heart Baptist church, a downtown Manhattan congregation that drew five thousand, even more, to three Sunday services. He'd kept the tan and the extra weight, and had mastered the tailored but understated wardrobe, and precisely barbered look, of the successful clergy man. Arlen the former lonely street preacher, imagine. The idea pleased Katie. Arlen always had good intentions, always followed the Lord's will as he saw it.

Bernie Smith was now a vice president of the union. His name was on the building directory in the prominent lettering granted senior executives. He arrived at monthly union meetings in a Cadillac Escalade and was as distinctively tailored and barbered as Arlen, except for the tie pin—perhaps a little too much glitter—and the mauve socks. On a television panel about city traffic, he called Mr. Kimmelman "Irving" and Mr. Kimmelman, with a thin diplomatic smile, called him "Bernie." How he must enjoy his new life, Katie reflected, happy with the thought. Bernie always had good intentions, too, in his way.

94

Leonard Swain. Well, to be fair, it really did look as if Katie was planting the tract on that snowy day outside the Shubert building. No begrudging him the Park Avenue office and the string of wealthy clients. Even his Foundation for Civic Freedom was earning praise in newspaper editorials and from the mayor himself, now that the bit of friction with the IRS was settled and a city-appointed manager installed. Small, balding men do have to push a little harder in this world, she conceded.

Then there was the tract itself. Arlen had been right. 'The Servant Heart' was read, reread, reprinted and talked about more than any tract since the time of Martin Luther. The content was unarguable, too. It offered no hellfire and brimstone, only stories of Christ's mercy and forgiveness spun around the gracious message of John 13:34.

"A new command I give you," Katie said aloud. "Love one another. As I have loved you, so you must love one another."

Some people would ridicule that, she thought. They ridiculed Jesus himself, after all. But with so many millions seeing those words, so many needing His love, many must have responded. How many? Even one made it worthwhile. Certainly the most valuable part of all that happened.

So it all turned out well, she repeated as she reached her post and eyed the row of low rise office buildings, the unhurried traffic.

Dusk was settling when she prepared to give her last ticket of the day to a new Chrysler Sebring, its showroom polish still glinting. It would be her sixth ticket, compared to fifty by this hour in a Manhattan tour. Alright, another Staten Island advantage, she admitted: nobody pushing her to meet a quota or dropping remarks about soft-hearted Katie.

The Sebring had one minute left. At the end of the day with offices closing down, the owner was sure to be on the way. She'd stroll to the corner and return, allowing a little overtime. A pack

The Marble King and Other Stories

of yellow legal pads on the front seat caught her eye as she passed. She stopped. About a dozen blue-covered stacks of papers, bound with brass clips, filled the rear seat.

Kathryn Dutton to the executive conference room...that terrifying day... the lawyers around the table...Mr. Kimmelman shaking a blue-covered stack of paper bound with brass clips at her...do you know what this is?

She did now.

Katie yanked the ticket writer from her belt. She angled the screen so she could read the timer clearly. She held her fingers poised.

The final second passed. For the first time in anyone's memory, including Katie's, her lower lip thrust out and her face pinched into sheer and deliberate spite. She punched the Violation button.

"Wait, please, I'm here," said a man's voice behind her.

Please don't be small and slightly balding came Katie's irrational thought.

It required a moment of effort. Then, spite erased, the guileless features of Katie Dutton back in their place, she turned to face a large, rather florid man with a blow dried mat of thick white hair. Katie took in an expensively tailored suit, shoes that gleamed like the Sebring, a wide, friendly smile and calculating eyes.

"I think we have a technicality here," he announced. "I arrived as the hour expired"—he indicated her timer—"so it's a matter of definition: does the violation start if the driver is at the car, and even more, is actually delayed by the parking officer's presence?" The smile widened and his voice lowered, growing confidential; they were in this together. "Then there's the question of intent. Courts always take that into account. I'm an attorney, by the way. My intent was clearly to move the car in keeping with the traffic code." He moved closer. "I spend a lot of time in court so I'm not a bad judge of people." He let the smile straighten into a thoughtful frown. "You, for example, just looking at you, tells me you're a forgiving person."

Leonard Swains come in all sizes, Katie thought.

Not the issue here, she instructed herself, not the issue at all, Kathryn.

Aloud, she said, "Let's consider this a warning, sir." She pressed Delete and hooked the ticket writer back on her belt.

"I truly appreciate that and I'll take the warning to heart, officer. You're the sort of public servant we need." He recaptured the friendly smile although unable to hide a split-second, victorious curl of his lips.

Yes, you outfoxed a dim witted meter maid, thought Katie.

I will pray that someday, somehow, you will understand this is not your victory.

It's mine.

She delayed going home after the Sebring left, drawn to the waterfront instead. She walked lightly, almost a little skip, trying hard to keep a more sober pace, murmuring, "Thank you, Lord, for protecting me from myself. Never again in spite, never again." Still conscious of her buoyant step, she finished, "With your help."

She regained her usual solid tread along the shoreline. She watched the gulls above, the boats on the bay and finally tested herself by staring at the Verrazano, measuring the slender span that reached Brooklyn and all that lay beyond.

Her shoulders moved up and down, slowly, calmly.

"Hey," she called to the gulls. "I take back that pigeon remark, okay?"

Stop me if you've heard this one. A lady executive from Milwaukee, a New York City fur designer and a kid from Harlem with a 175 IQ walk into a chess center…

The Vienna Game

Mona spent a moment fighting the impulse, gave in and followed the boy carrying the black drawstring bag into the park. She caught up to him just inside the entrance.

"I'm sorry to bother you but I'm curious." She pointed to the bag. "Where do you play chess here?"

The boy, college age, stared for no more than a second at the six foot tall, fifty-five year old woman facing him, noting the cross at her neck, not registering her five thousand dollar wardrobe. Mona was content with that. In Milwaukee, she would have been inspected like a museum exhibit.

"On a hill by the skating rink." He pointed. "Do your kids play?"

"I have no children. I play. Or I did, many years ago."

"That the Kasparov book of openings?" He touched a small, hardcover volume in her hand. "Got some useful stuff."

"It's a book of Psalms and Proverbs. Also got some useful stuff."

He ignored that. "The dark cover, looks like the Kasparov. Anyway, you go up the hill by the rink. You can borrow chess pieces if you don't bring your own."

She watched him walk off, leaned willowlike toward the path and turned away. Ten minutes later, she gazed out her apartment window, absorbing the view of the park across Fifth Avenue. This sight alone made moving here worthwhile. She tried to picture the chess tables hidden somewhere inside the greenery and winding paths.

Don't even think about it, she told herself. She was an eternity away from the nine year old who walked to school clutching a chessboard, chin high as her father had advised, sailing through the schoolyard insults and taunts. She had found something she was good at, better than the others, not easy for a girl so large, so ungainly.

She proved herself. School champion, regional champion, state champion, the only girl in the contests, self-confident, yes, enough self-confidence now to deflect the remarks, enough to make the loneliness bearable through high school and university.

Then business replaced chess. With her father's death, the company was hers to manage. The first conference with the lawyers and directors felt like the schoolyard again. Remarks about her youth, her lack of experience, the heavy competition, the complexity of the business were, in her ears, the old insults and taunts. One elderly director with a kindly smile suggested a career in a religious organization, knowing how devout her family was. An executive committee would manage the business for her.

She said mildly, "Please send me a written proposal for a committee and its purposes."

Somehow, after two years, the proposal was still in preparation. Mona asked for a revision here, suggested a subcommittee there, requested some research on this point, needed a clarification on that point. The two years also saw over-familiar faces vanish from key departments and fresh ones appear, one at a time, decent intervals in between each change, nothing that resembled a purge.

The smarter lawyers and directors realized, admiringly, that they had received a lesson in life as a chess game. The others swallowed their complaints. The company was prospering under Mona's management. Why meddle with it?

Mona discovered that "the hill by the skating rink" was actually a cliff-like outpost of bedrock north of the rink and overlooking it. Reaching it, expecting a sunbaked little plateau with a few weathered wooden tables and benches, Mona stopped in surprise. A sheltered retreat lay before her, an enclave of at least two dozen well scrubbed and rugged stone tables surrounding a small red brick cottage. This would be the place where chess pieces could be borrowed, with Hansel and Gretel among the borrowers by the look of it. A leafy trellis around and over the tables filtered out sunlight and the sounds of the busy park. Benches painted a deep summer green completed the arbor-like setting.

Inside, of course, the charm took on an edge. Little Coliseums, Mona thought, stirring despite herself to the sounds of combat—the slap and counter slap of pieces planted on their squares and the sword-like *chingk!* of chess clocks timing each player's moves. Blood lust at my age, she scolded, strolling easily along, trying to appear uninterested, just a tourist passing through. She missed nothing, though, happily taking in table after table of chessmen pursuing, assaulting, capturing across their checkered battlegrounds; taking in the players, too, the frowns, the scowls, the squints, the knit brows—the ever present facial language of a game grounded, from its first move, in tension.

The lone exception was a heavy set man of perhaps sixty with close-cut iron grey hair, gazing calmly at the board, hands clasped stolidly on the table, shoulders resting easily against the slatted back of the bench. Mona recognized the manner as her own. "Conceal your reactions," her father had instructed. "Your opponent can learn from them. And you can learn from his."

The strategy hardly seemed necessary here. The man's opponent, a black boy wearing a Riverside Christian Academy jacket, bounced up and down and scuttled side to side across his bench without a break. He appeared about middle school age and Mona recalled the rigid posture training of her own childhood. Muscles ached at the memory. Do some bouncing for me, young man.

She headed back toward the rink, pleased. An enjoyable interlude although she wouldn't play here. She had spotted only one female among the players, a wild-haired, mid-thirties woman flashing rings on every finger, muttering steadily to herself. One eccentric woman was enough. They didn't need an aging Valkyrie swathed in custom-tailored silk. She had digested her bit of chess nostalgia and that was that.

She sat reading by the carousel the next day, across the roadway from the skating rink, when a flock of pigeons began their strutting and throaty calling around her feet. It usually amused her. Today, for some reason, it was annoying. Time to go back to her apartment, anyway. She rose, intending to head south, the shortest way to Fifth Avenue, finding herself eastbound instead, passing the rink. It's a prettier path, she told herself, admitting the lie when she reached the hill and started up. One more look, why not?

She walked by the tables a little slower this time, satisfied that players were focused on their games, paying no attention to her. She paused momentarily here and there to check a position, resisting the urge to linger at the better games. The lone woman was there again, muttering away, although the relaxed man with the iron grey hair was absent.

That's the end of it, she told herself resolutely on the way home. Enough time wasted. I have better things to do.

In her circuit of the tables the next day, she immersed herself in the moves of a particularly tense contest, one that would keep all eyes on the board without a glance at her. Twice she saw better moves than those made by the players. She scanned the other onlookers. Their expressions told her none of them had seen what she had. Pleased, she walked on, her mind still probing the position and its possibilities, unable to stop, the true chess player's addiction.

A voice broke in near the exit. "Hey, Yellow Dress, over here."

The man with the iron grey hair was pointing at the chess board. His opponent, the same boy, bounced around as before without turning to look at her.

After three decades as a company CEO, addressed as Ms. Mc-Cormick or Madam Chairwoman or Ma'am, she blinked at Yellow Dress, momentarily offended.

"I know, I know," he said. "But it was either Yellow Dress or Hey Babe. You're not a Hey Babe. Anyway, my name is Mortie, Mortie Greenberg." He followed with a shrug and a lift of the eyebrows that said, So? What can I do about it?

She walked to the table, vaguely flattered and wondering why. She dismissed the nagging awareness of her size and her gamble on wearing yellow today instead of a camouflaging darker color. He was not asking for a date.

"Mona McCormick," she said.

"A Greenberg meets a McCormick. Some names are labels." He tapped the bench beside him with such casual assurance Mona sat down even as a flicker of resentment struck. *Come here. Sit down.* Madam Chairwoman the lap dog?

103

The Marble King and Other Stories

"This is Rafael Sands," Mortie was saying.

"No label here. Black daddy, Peurto Rican mommy." He waved a finger in rhythm like a baton and chanted, "Hey, I'm a dozen years old, with an IQ off the chart, wanna give a label, you can label me real smart." He looked up and aimed a grin at her. "What are you reading? Would a twelve year old genius like it?"

"Psalms and Proverbs, books of the Bible. Even a genius can learn from them."

"You carry it all the time?"

"I carry it on days when I want to sit peacefully and meditate, sort of sweeping things that don't matter out of your mind—"

"I know what meditate means. I know the Bible, too. Moses. Let my people go. Jesus. Love and forgive. Samson. Give me a new do. Jonah. What am I, bait?" He returned his attention to the chessboard.

"Rafael," said Mortie.

The boy stared at the board. Mortie held up a hand for Mona's benefit. Wait.

Some ten seconds or so elapsed. Eyes still lowered, the boy murmured, "Yeah, I know." His gaze lifted and he said, "I'm sorry, Mortie."

He turned to Mona. "I apologize. I respect the Bible. I'm going to read it a lot." He patted the Riverside Christian Academy patch on his back. "I respect you. Should I call you Mrs. McCormick?"

"It would be *Ms* McCormick. Mona's good, though." She surprised herself with that. Casual use of first names usually displeased her. The surroundings, she decided.

The grin reappeared, accompanied by a deliberate wrinkle of his nose while the eyes remained dark and serious. He looked down again at the board, leaving Mona regarding thick black curls.

THE VIENNA GAME

"Don't fall in love," Mortie said. "He's a charmer. But look"—he swept a hand over the chessboard—"this is why I called you over."

She scanned the position.

"I see the sixth or seventh move in a French Defense. Routine. What am I missing?"

He wagged a bishop back and forth. "Sha, sha, sha, Mona McCormick. How old is that book of yours?" He leaned toward her so he could lift the cover and ruffle a few pages, his fingers careful and precise with the yellowing paper, his heavy shoulder pressing against hers as he reached.

You resent this familiarity, Mona, she told herself.

"It was a gift when I started high school."

"Okay, forty years give or take. It's been rebound by an expert, I can tell, so you care for vintage things."

"I see what you're trying to—"

"Then there's the yellow dress. Tells me a lot. This is beyond the Balenciagas of the world. This is from one of those elderly ladies you learn about in select circles, only in whispers, don't let it get around, my dear—lives in a rent-controlled apartment somewhere, a Rembrandt with a needle"—he ran a thumb over an invisible stitch at her neck—"a sense of design to hide here, to emphasize there"—his hands made curves in the air—"and the price? Three thousand? Five thousand? A bargain when you appreciate the finer things, which you do. Now, what do you see on the board? And not just the position. That can be hypnotic, I know—"

"Will you please stop talking?" It was crisp, the CEO voice.

"Why not?" Mortie said placidly.

"Times you want to whack him upside the head," remarked Rafael, sliding a pawn forward.

105

The Marble King and Other Stories

"I see wooden pieces that were not borrowed," Mona said. "These were turned on a bench with the knights finely detailed by a molding process. They're based on a horse's head sculpture in the British Museum's Elgin collection. The British Chess Company made these between the late Eighteen Hundreds and early Nineteen Hundreds. The dark patina of this set tells me it's from the earliest years. So do the slightly elongated king and queen." She touched the two pieces lightly. "Hard to find these sets now. Congratulations. Do you need to know more? The sizes they came in? The turn of the century prices?"

"Thank you," said Mortie. "That takes care of what you see. Now tell me what you don't see."

"And what I don't hear." She waved at the ringing sound of chess clocks at other tables. "No clock at this table. You find yourself in this little bower here, a sanctuary in its way, but with assembly line plastic pieces all around you and the clocks rushing you along. It makes chess like driving a freeway. So you pretend you're in an English garden, playing as they did in days gone by, games that could last twelve hours. You're a throwback, a romantic."

Did I sound that smug at board meetings, she wondered. Well, what of it?

"So you're from out of town," was Mortie's only comment . "New Yorkers don't say freeways. They're expressways here."

"You call that romantic talk?" Rafael asked. "Your move, Mortie."

"She meant romantic in the historic sense, someone who idealizes the past."

"Okay, no mushy mushy. Still your move."

Mortie picked up a rook, examined it, held it up so the sun glinted off the polished wood, rolled it lovingly in his fingers—yes, I get the point, I'm going to punch you, thought Mona— and

106

set it on a new file. A series of six moves and countermoves unreeled with Rafael responding almost instantly to Mortie's play. Mona recognized that despite his bouncing around the boy had been picturing and analyzing this entire sequence. It was an impressive display by anyone, let alone a twelve year old.

The game was now in its middle stage, with both armies fully engaged and the need for concentration at its peak. Mona watched the players as much as the board, her tournament habits instinctively coming into play. Mortie had resumed his serene face while Rafael stayed himself. He bounced, pursed his lips, made clucking noises, pointed fingers like pistols at Mortie, shook his head in disdain, even kept up a little patter. "That the best you can do?" "You call that a chess move?" "Oh, you're cooked now." "You just made a bad choice, my friend." "Here's a move that'll wipe that smile off your face."

Mortie did smile at that, the first crack in a Buddha-like mask that Mona was no longer trying to read. After fifteen minutes, she had discovered a little patch of stubble at Mortie's jaw missed by his razor, eyebrows with an interesting mix of black and grey, a ruddy complexion with none of the splotches or veins of the drinker, so common at his age, and hazel eyes—or brown? Hard to see from the side.

But of telltale signs, nothing. He was as practiced as she was. Face, hands, torso, all at rest, revealed neither satisfaction nor concern, although the course of the game now called for satisfaction. Mortie had skillfully built a kingside pawn attack backed by a bishop and took pointed at the heart of Rafael's defense. If the boy was good, Mortie was close to master level, playing with a style she once dismissed as bricklaying—a patient, square by square construction of a winning position.

Having been beaten now and then by such bricklayers, she had learned to appreciate the skill involved, although she had never altered her own slashing, adventurous way at the board. The most memorable games came from that clash of styles. She and Mortie could play enjoyable matches. She was the better player, she observed—Rafael had missed parries to Mortie's moves that she would have spotted—but the games would be close. He'd improve after a few games, too, the Proverbs 27:17 effect: *As iron sharpens iron, one person sharpens another.*

"Yeah, yeah, yeah, beat up on a helpless child, what do you care," Rafael said, turning his king over in defeat.

"What did the helpless child learn?" Mortie asked.

"If you're going to play a French Defense, keep the white bishop off here." He pointed.

"Good, that's progress."

"Not quite enough," Mona added, reaching past Mortie to shuffle pieces. "A pawn here, or a knight here, early on, fourth or fifth move, and the rook can't line up on you later. Do you see it?"

"Hey, that's cool. You can play this game! Mortie, she's a real chess player."

"I knew that."

"You telepathic now? We just met her."

"I saw the way she watched the other games."

Mona lectured herself about the yellow dress. She must have stood out like Macy's Big Bird balloon. The dark blue next time, the tailored look—no, forget a next time.

"Cool. She'll whump you good," Rafael said, picking up a book bag from beneath the bench. "Tomorrow, you're deprived. No Rafael. Stupid state exams, all day."

"I'll be calling the school," Mortie told him. "You better be there." To Mona, he explained, "Summer school, to make up for his truancy during the regular season." Turning back to Rafael, he added, "Not only be there, be there on time."

"Like Lincoln never lived," Rafael said. He trudged off with deliberately heavy steps, book bag balanced on his head, a plantation worker.

"Gaining ground," Mortie said, satisfaction plain in his voice. He began to pack the chess pieces in a varnished box, thick fingers quickly stacking the intricate shapes so they fit the confines of the box exactly. She always needed two or three tries to get it right.

"He used to fight with me about school attendance," Mortie went on. "Now, just a little teasing. And he's able to apologize when he knows he's wrong, the way he did with you." He rotated muscular shoulders in a slow stretch and pushed himself up from the bench. "So, Mona McCormick, from out of town. May one inquire where?"

"Milwaukee. Now you'll ask me why trade Milwaukee for New York. Everybody does."

He spread his palms. I'm not everybody. I don't insist.

That was annoying somehow.

"I ran a business in Milwaukee and I knew I couldn't retire there. They'd keep dragging me back for this problem or that. I needed distance."

He cocked his head, waiting. His palms were still raised, telling her this is up to you, but we both know that's a contrived answer. Irritation flared and subsided for Mona as she regarded the massive man before her. Standing now, he was revealed as no taller than she was but a tank of a man side to side, overweight in the way some wrestlers are, bulk without flab.

And he was right about her answer. She fought down irritation again. Why did I even respond at all? Why give a stranger license to pry?

He seemed to sense her thoughts. "Okay," he said, "I'll tell you something. When I went to high school, I went where all my friends went. When I chose a college, I chose one where none of my friends went. You get the point. Clean slate. No friends by circumstance—the neighborhood, the classroom, the workplace—instead, solitude, which can have its rewards, or new friends by choice, not circumstance. Am I right about you, Mona McCormick?"

When she hesitated, he said, "Greenbergs are always right. It's in the DNA." Then, startling Mona, he broke into a little shuffling dance, clapping his hands, sliding sideways, humming a Hebrew melody off key. "Yes?" he asked when he stopped.

Hasty glances around assured Mona the players were all absorbed in their games. "That's hardly any help. You are not one of those big men who dances gracefully. It's embarrassing."

"It's not embarrassing. It's Central Park. And deep down, you enjoy it. This freedom—it's why you fled Milwaukee." He started clapping again.

"You're oversimplifying. And that's enough ballet for one day." It sounded severe, more than she intended.

"Ah, I see. Oversimplifying. A man is involved. No more questions, then."

Mona caught her breath. *He thinks enough of me to imagine I could have a love affair. Well, yes, and more than one, just not what he imagines. But bless him for imagining it.*

"So we laugh the sorrow away. Or we dance it away, yes?" He started the clapping again.

"Enough teasing," she cautioned. "I think Rafael is not the only adolescent I met today."

"Ah, Rafael." He took the box of chessmen from the table and absent mindedly shook it. "Gaining ground," he said, this time thoughtfully, and added nothing else. Seeing the sobering of mood, Mona stayed silent, too. They went through the exit and started down the hill, still quiet. At the paths leading out of the park, Mortie said, "I'm going to the West Side, to the subway. I have a class to teach, something you do when you retire. I'll tell you about Rafael when we meet for chess tomorrow. Noon, yes? I'll pick up lunch. Roast beef sandwiches, kosher dill pickle, root beer. Something else sound better?" He was smiling, a little forced. Rafael was still on his mind.

"That sounds fine," Mona said, pleased and not pleased. So she would be there for chess. An assumption, not an invitation, not a choice. Well, at least she had approval rights with the sandwiches. Thank you, Mortie.

After they parted, a sudden thought brought her around. "What do you teach?" she called.

"Fur design. I was the city's premier designer. Some say the world's." He was completely in earnest.

The third time Mortie asked if the sandwiches were alright, she said, "They're delicious, I'm satisfied, and I would tell you if they weren't. I'm not shy."

"No, not any more. Takes a lot of years, though, doesn't it?" His hand moved across his chest, indicating his size.

Yes, and mine by implication, Mona understood. Outsized people like us, different, lonely, targeted. She tipped the root beer bottle to her mouth, looking up at the trellised leaves, trying to hide the anger. You are not my father, my brother, my lover. I don't need such an intimate bond from someone I met only yesterday! Do you expect me to be grateful? For reminding me we're sideshow attractions together?

Mortie evidently expected nothing. The board held his attention, not Mona, and she understood his remark was not intended to establish anything between them. It merely affirmed a bond already there, an even greater claim of intimacy than she had supposed.

This is insane, she protested, the thought slipping away at the sight of Mortie's face, now in its deliberately stoic chess mode, eyes steady on the bishop's pawn she had pushed ahead. The move steered them into the Vienna Game, a bold line of play more than a century old and a secret weapon for the few adept with it. Played well, the Vienna would see Mona's queen dominating the board. It was her favorite system and she had once savored, then shrugged off the Freudian overtones.

Mortie played smartly, surprising her by abandoning the bricklayer style of his game with Rafael, making a risky foray with a knight and his own queen that hemmed in her queen and made her scramble for a defense. She found it, counter-attacked and slowly forced a pawn and rook ending with a one pawn advantage, enough to win. Ironically, she had to adopt the square by square method herself against Mortie's stubborn resistance.

Amusement replaced serenity in Mortie's expression as he turned down his king. His eyes—they were hazel—rolled upward in a "Why me?" expression before settling on Mona. He tried to look accusing.

"The Vienna Game. Was that fair?"

"You like things from the past. You'll have first move next time, your choice of opening."

Now *she* was doing it. Next time, taken for granted. Mona, where is your head?

"Probably won't help me, the way you play. Will you teach the Vienna to Rafael tomorrow? He'll jump off the bench with joy. About three o'clock, after school. By the way, blue's a good color for you." He reached for his root beer, then added, "Three alright?"

THE VIENNA GAME

Well! Finally some recognition that my day is not at your disposal. And yes, blue works for me. That's why I wore it.

"It's alright, but tell me about Rafael. All that truancy—he's not getting along at Riverside Christian?"

"He doesn't go there. He wants to. It's a great school and I'm trying to help."

"The jacket?"

"Won in a chess game from some unsuspecting kid in Bryant Park. Rafael's an accomplished chess hustler, of course. He was playing hooky from the school he does attend when he feels like it, a public school in Harlem."

"No supervision? His parents?"

"He's an orphan. Father liked motorcycles, hit a patch of oil on the Bronx Expressway one night. Mother, two years later, breast cancer. She was only thirty-five. Rafael was six. He's in a foster home now with a flock of other kids. Rafael has a bed and meals. Otherwise, he's on his own."

"Where did you meet him?"

Mortie laughed. "Right here. He sat down beside me and said 'You've been chosen.' I said, 'Thousands of years ago.' He needed a second, then said, 'Oh, the Jews. You're a funny guy. We'll get along. Now you've been chosen again, this time by Rafael Sands, me, to improve my game. I'll owe you a quarter for each lesson. Non-negotiable. We can start now.'"

"And you started."

"Was there an option?" His smile at the memory came and faded. He fiddled absently with one of the pieces.

"It's beyond chess lessons now, isn't it?" Mona prompted. "You call the school to check up on him."

"I'm trying to adopt him," Mortie said.

Mona was not as surprised as he seemed to expect. "Can you do that?"

113

"I'm a sixty-one year old widower who lives alone, not your typical adopter. I don't know. I have a lawyer at work on it."

"How does Rafael feel about it?"

Mortie's smile returned. "When I told him, he said, 'No way you get a chance to be on my case twenty-four seven, take away all my freedom. You see me going around calling you Poppa? You gonna walk me to school, hold my hand? Ain't never gonna happen!'"

"That means he's willing," Mona said.

"The next second, he asked how far I lived from Riverside Christian. A ten-minute bus ride, I told him. 'Too far, man,' he answered. 'We gotta move.' He gave me that grin of his."

"So he's more than willing. But this school, why is he so eager to go there? A Christian academy will have a dress code, strict rules, demanding class work, a tightly ordered environment."

Mortie just looked at her.

"Oh. The wounded animal knows what it needs."

"When he won the jacket he got curious. He peeked in the windows, listened to the kids coming and going, even walked right into the office and asked for their brochures. You know Rafael. He got them, practically memorized them. He understands the school."

Mortie started packing the chess pieces in the box, fingers moving slowly this time. "There's something else. My lawyer says it will help the adoption process if he goes there. A private academy, the high standards—the court is influenced when a child has a chance at such an elite school. The cost impresses them, too. Judges are only human. They want to see a fund set up that will guarantee the tuition. Twenty-five thousand a year. Rafael has six years to go, so you're dealing with one hundred fifty thousand, probably more as rates go up."

He placed the last piece in the box, looked at her and said "Crazy world. A child's future comes with a price tag." He closed the lid, snapping the latch to make sure it was tight. "Come, I have to get to my class now."

She nodded. They walked down the hill, Mortie chatting about the rigorous entrance exams for the school and the family interview—how will I handle that?—and the possibility that Rafael could set new academic records there. As they separated, he said, "Tomorrow, then."

"I may not be able to make it," Mona answered. She caught his perplexed look as she walked off.

Standing again at the apartment window, she pulled the shade to cut off her view of the park.

One more time, the money. A designer, he would have noticed the exclusive outfit from afar. Hey, Yellow Dress, over here. Bring your checkbook. I know, his manner, so straightforward, there's no imitating that. It is truly the way he is. Fresh air after the oily fog of over-educated fakers—why did she seem to attract college professors?—but the same object. "Ah, I see," he had said. "There's a man involved." It's *men*, Mortie, plural, multiple, pursuing, pretending, proposing, then spiteful and spreading lies when they're turned away. You wouldn't believe the silliness of it. A woman smart enough to earn a fortune suddenly dumb enough to trade it for a little rehearsed flattery? Greed is blinding, isn't it?

I understand, greed is not a factor here. There's a chance to help a child who deserves it. I'll take care of that. But Mortie, pure motive or not, the money has always been in your mind, hasn't it?

In the morning, Mona visited the treasurer of Parkway Baptist, her church. She arranged for Parkway to pay the first year for Rafael and pledge the remaining years. Her name would not be associated with it in any way. She filled the rest of the day with volunteer work at the church, resetting bulletin boards, arranging Sunday School rooms, then dinner at a quiet East Side restaurant and a concert at Lincoln Center. That was Friday.

The following Thursday when Mona returned home after a day of museum visits, the desk man handed her an envelope. A large man and a boy, black and with an impudent look, had left it.

Upstairs, she made herself a pot of tea, changed clothes and sat quietly to pray, asking for wisdom and peace of mind and reciting from the psalm, "In you, Oh Lord, do I put my trust; let me never be put to confusion." She took the letter, finally, from her purse.

Dear Mona McCormick,

In some way, I offended you. I have puzzled over it and now conclude it was the remark about blue being a good color for you. Did you think it meant I was criticizing the yellow dress? Well, to be candid, I was. The cut and styling were superb but yellow? No. Furs come in a variety of dyes and tints today, so I have had to develop a professional eye for such things. Blue, particularly dark blues, are flattering for you. Dark green and maroon are other good choices. You might experiment with deep lavender. I have enclosed a color chart that I use with my design classes.

Please understand that this, and my remark, are intended to be helpful. I realize I am making a judgment about your wardrobe sense but it is my specialty, my Vienna Game. Criticism of you, as a person, is absolutely not intended.

In friendship, and hoping for more chess games,

Mordecai H. Greenberg

Mona examined her teacup without seeing it. Do I cry? Do I scream? Do I laugh? I finally meet an honest man and it gets me a fashion lecture, plus "criticism of you, as a person, is absolutely not intended." Does it mean that praise of me, as a person, *is* absolutely intended? Is a color chart the equivalent of a dozen roses, an apology?

Perspective, Mona. Nothing has changed. He wouldn't know yet that Rafael's tuition is paid, so it's important to keep the channel open. In his own Mordecai Greenberg way. Why can't he be completely deceitful? I could deal with that. And why must Rafael be so appealing? "I'll owe you a quarter for each game. Non negotiable."

She sighed, tore the letter and chart in two and dropped them in the wastebasket. Then she reached in and tore them into shreds.

On Tuesday, another envelope. Time to stop, Mortie.

Dear Mona McCormick,

Rafael passed his entrance exams at Riverside Christian. Actually, he achieved some of the highest scores in their history. I'm hesitant to impose on you but there is still one matter in which he could use your help. I'm guessing that you care about him despite any problem between us. This help will be needed by next Friday.

Thank you for considering this request,

Mordecai H. Greenberg
22 East 12th Street
735-0204.

She would call the church treasurer first thing in the morning. Mortie must be informed about the payment. The note went into the wastebasket.

Instead, the treasurer called her that evening, full of regrets for being out of touch so long. He had been away at a missions conference, followed by a much needed vacation and was working late, catching up on the mail. He wanted her to know that Riverside Christian had returned the check, explaining that an account was already established for Rafael Sands by his sponsor, a Mr. Greenberg, covering all six years of tuition.

Mona resisted the impulse to go for a walk. The business years had taught her that troublesome situations must be faced immediately. She reclaimed the note, readied her answers to his inevitable questions and dialed the number.

"Mortie Greenberg here."

"This is Mona McCormick. Will you be playing chess tomorrow?"

"At noon, yes."

"I'd like to meet you there."

He paused, a second, no more, then, "Corned beef sandwiches this time? From the Carnegie Deli. Best in the city. They cure the beef themselves and carve it for each order on the spot, no lying around in a steam table, couldn't be fresher. Nothing like it in Milwaukee, guaranteed."

"Yes, it sounds good. Thank you."

She hung up and stared at the phone.

Mordecai H. Greenberg.

No questions.

Just corned beef sandwiches.

Also color charts.

THE VIENNA GAME

Rafael stood on the bench and raised his fists in a victory salute when she appeared. "Mona, Mona, Mona, thought you'd gone to Arizona! Wanna know why I'm so pumped up to see you? I need a friend. Mortie's a drill sergeant. Gets me up before dawn—"

"Eight o'clock. The sun's shining."

"Back in bed in the afternoon—"

"Nine P.M."

"You're together now?" Mona asked. "The adoption?"

"Will be formalized next month," Mortie answered. "I have foster parent status until then."

"Right," Rafael said. "You're on probation. Start treating me better or I walk."

"Not a problem. I buy a beagle puppy to replace you."

Rafael started to giggle. He bounced on the bench.

"No way! They don't come in black!"

Rafael's giggle turned into a fit and Mortie's big frame rocked from side to side. They pointed at each other triumphantly.

After they subsided, Mortie said, "Okay, no beagle, but you're on a leash. I need to talk to Mona seriously."

"Wants you to play mommy," Rafael said.

A caution signal went on for Mona.

"Mouth zipped," Mortie told Rafael. To Mona, he said, "Friday is the family interview. If they have questions about material things, that's easy. But questions about spiritual things? I'm lost there. Will I take him to church? Have him baptized? Other questions a Mortie Greenberg can't even think of?"

He leaned over the table toward her. "I took a chance. I asked if I could bring along a close friend, a Christian lady who wants to help. It's a presumption, I know. I'll understand if you can't do it. It's a presumption," he repeated, then broke into a tentative smile at her expression.

119

The Marble King and Other Stories

"See?" said Rafael. "She's happy about it. Look at her. You gotta listen to me."

Get control, Mona, she warned herself, before you resemble a Halloween pumpkin.

"I want to do it," she told Mortie. "Very much."

He clapped his hands in rhythm and moved as if to stand up.

She shook her head and he sat back. "Too bad," he said. "It's a nice day for some tribal dancing."

"Nicer day for lunch," said Rafael, sniffing energetically toward the box on Mortie's bench.

They ate contentedly, Mona praising the sandwiches before Mortie could ask, Rafael claiming it was his first good meal in a week, Mortie snorting at the idea, Rafael admitting maybe since breakfast, the man can cook up an alright waffle, who'd believe?

When they finished, Mortie looked purposefully at Rafael.

"I know, this is the time I take that little walk," Rafael said. "Secret grownup stuff going down now."

"You've got your ice cream money?" Mortie asked.

"I'll give it back if I can stay."

Mortie waved in the direction of the park's creamery.

"Alright. But listen, we've already done the first two steps of my plan. She's coming to the meeting, she can take me to church. Now you've got to—"

"Rafael, go!"

"On my way." Words tumbled out, addressed to Mona. "Way I see it, he tells you about Mrs. Mortie who died, we do something with your money so it doesn't bug us, we settle on whose apartment, we convert Mortie little by little, a lot of deep stuff to get through, but you know how Bobby Fischer became champion?" He tapped the chess board. "One move at a time. I'm going."

He skipped off, flapping his arms. At the exit, he turned and called, "Be mature about this."

Mortie rubbed his eyes, then brushed his hands back and forth through his close cropped hair. Mona looked after Rafael, trying to let the flush leave her face.

"An IQ of one hundred seventy five," Mortie said. "But still twelve years old." He opened the box of chessmen and began to set them up. He waved at Mona's dress with a knight.

"Teal green, today. Nice, soft shade. You didn't need any advice from me, did you? Mortie, I told myself over and over, you're a dunce. Why did you ever make that remark?"

"The remark never bothered me. I knew you were right. It was something else."

"Ah? What then?"

When she finished, he nodded, face tight with anger. "To treat you so badly, these, these maggots." He slammed a huge fist into a palm, then inhaled, a long, deep breath that expanded his chest like an ocean swell. He let it out slowly and said, "I understand why you would be so suspicious of me, anybody. I never thought to explain the tuition. To me, it was obvious I would pay."

"And to me it was obvious a fur designer, even the best, wouldn't have that sort of money. I don't know anything about furs. I avoid them. A fur would make me look like a wooly mammoth."

He lifted his hand like a traffic cop. "You'll have a Greenberg design and your mind will change. Non negotiable," he added as she began to protest. "Anyway, the top designers make one hundred thousand a year. I was twice as good as top. Many years, three times." There was nothing boastful in his words. The sun rises in the East. Simple fact.

"And I lived frugally," he added. "Chess players are cautious people. Have you ever known a chess player to live recklessly?"

"Are you serious? Adopting a high spirited child when you're sixty-one? Maybe just a little reckless?"

The shrug came again, the lift of the eyebrows, the gesture when he first told her his name. So? What can I do about it?

Mona felt a wave of merriment rising. Where had that come from?

"And playing against the Vienna Game. Now that's reckless." She made it a challenge, letting the mood wash over her.

"You're daring me? Another Vienna Game? Go ahead, try it."

She picked up the king's pawn and slapped it down two squares ahead, trying to look pugnacious, unable to control the corners of her mouth.

At the ninth move, she heard a faint humming sound from Mortie. His lower lip was thrust forward, his brow furrowed, puzzling over where to go next.

And she had her cheeks puffed out while her eyes stabbed here and there at the board, revealing the same uncertainty.

We've been playing the whole game this way, she realized.

Rafael sat down next to her, holding the remains of an over-sized chocolate cone. His head swiveled from Mortie to Mona and back again.

"You guys aren't doing poker face with each other? Hey!" He jumped up in excitement, then sat down with deliberate calm. "This is really the third step of my plan. Didn't tell you about it. Knew you'd figure it out yourselves."

"Rafael," said Mortie. "Listen to me. Mona and I are friends. We play chess. That's a very good thing. No more with the plan."

"Right," he said. He muttered so only Mona could hear, "Move at a time."

What a blessing it is when your wife is always right…

Front Matter

Des considered his wife with the affection forty years of a sweet marriage will bring. Also with the alertness forty years of a sweet marriage will bring. The way the slightest touch of a northeast wind starts a mariner searching the sky, the little line between her brows sent him searching her face—okay, no real stress showing, no major squall coming, just—something.

He tried to make out where she was in the Bible she held open—they sat opposite at a table in the screened porch, a cypress rustling overhead—and she was at the very beginning of the book. What could be troubling in Genesis? It wasn't James, a book that made you re-examine yourself and actually, with a closer look, he saw she hadn't even reached Genesis. It was the front matter, those pages before the text that people never notice unless, like Des, you had worked in publishing. He angled his head for a better look—strange, it was the page right inside the front cover, the blank, protective one that people use for a message if the book is a gift —

The Marble King and Other Stories

Ah, that.

A sheet from a small office note pad had been carefully pasted there, a page imprinted Mount Roanoke Assisted Living, with the hand-written inscription, *From Nurse Sarah To Mrs. Peterson, Here's God's Precious Word, With Love.*

At the time she had shown it to him, it meant nothing. You buy a used book, you save money in return for wear and tear and somebody else's notations.

The Bible, an English Standard Version his wife was trying out—they were New International Version readers by habit—had been ordered online from !READ! the national book service, and fulfilled by one of the independent stores in its network.

"It's pilfered," she said.

Well, that was a simple issue to address.

"Can you pilfer a Bible? As a philosophical matter, it's God's word, meant to be disseminated, so even theft is a good thing."

She turned thoughtful and opened to Genesis.

The following day at breakfast, she told Des, "Maybe." After enough years of marriage, a loose thread of conversation can be picked up with a word. "It doesn't change the fact that I can't hold this book without thinking of Mrs. Peterson in Assisted Living. That could be us but for the grace of God. It's her Bible, not mine, and it's a gift from an employee. How many employees give gifts to the people they work for? It must be a very loving relationship and whoever pilfered it didn't even read it, just sold it. How much can you get for a used book, anyhow?"

"Well, assume the book is only part of wholesale petty thievery by someone, so in a week, maybe enough for a few packs of cigarettes or a jug of cheap wine."

"Or worse."

"Or worse. Or maybe better. Food for a hungry family."

126

"Like Les Miserables? They didn't have food stamps and food pantries and school lunches. You're just being protective, trying to keep me from being bothered."

"What's wrong with that? And you shouldn't be bothered. There's nothing you can do about it."

She turned her attention to a scrambled egg on her plate and any outside observer would suppose the matter was settled, but Des had seen the furrow deepen a little. He felt another little brush of the northeast wind and remembered the apartment incident.

Out on a Sunday stroll some thirty-five years ago in New York City, in need of an apartment at a time when vacancies had three month waiting lists, they walked past an uncommonly well kept apartment building on University Place, a prime city location. She stopped to examine the management plaque, repeating the name and address, memorizing it.

"That's an exercise in futility," he said. "Save yourself the disappointment. Nobody calls a management company cold these days and gets an apartment. They'll laugh at you."

The next afternoon, they were signing the lease. She displayed no triumph, not a hint of 'I told you so,' only innocent contentment.

So *There's nothing you can do about it* was probably not the smartest answer, but what other answer was there; what could she do about it?

At dinnertime, she said, "I emailed !READ! this afternoon. I asked if pilfered books were sold through their stores or if they had some safeguards against it."

They'll never answer went through his mind. He said nothing and congratulated himself on his wisdom.

!READ! answered the next day with the candid admission, Yes, pilfered books probably do show up in the inventories of our participating stores since there's no way to check on whether books are acquired licitly. People lose, discard, trade or give books to others by the million.

Alright, Des thought, this closes the book, so to speak, on this episode.

She was writing a letter the following morning when Des looked out to the porch, to her sister, Des assumed, something she did regularly and something that pleased the retired book publisher in him in this day of quick and thoughtless cyber-talk.

He saw wrapping paper on the table, so she'd be sending some sort of gift to her sister, too—an assumption that evaporated when he saw her wrap the Bible.

"I looked up the Mount Roanoke address. I'm sending this back to Mrs. Peterson with a letter explaining why."

"You are one persistent woman," he said. "With initiative. I'm pleased." And he was; the matter was finally solved and she would be at ease.

"I ordered another one from !READ! for us," she said.

"Sure you're not taking a chance?"

"We can buy more wrapping paper."

A letter came the following week from a Mrs. Alice Beale, Mrs. Peterson's daughter. Mrs. Peterson had passed on three months ago and her sight failed near the end so she, Mrs. Beale, had read to her each day from this Bible. It was a reminder of that time and a book she treasured. God bless you, she wrote, what a fine Christian woman you are!

Des found himself teary-eyed along with his wife. And humbled, he confessed to himself, by the way things had worked out despite his skepticism.

When the replacement Bible arrived from !Read! the first thing they did was check the inside front cover page and there was no gift inscription –

"Good!" she said.

128

— because there was no inside front cover page. The cover opened directly to what book-producers call the half-title page, where just the name of the book is presented, without the author's name or other information. Most people don't care about front matter. Most people would never notice the missing page.

A retired publisher would, and did.

But I am not going to get my magnifying glass and worklight and examine it for deliberate removal, Des told himself. It's a book manufacturing error. Or a book designer's decision.

He studied it under the worklight while his wife slept that night and there, clear in the magnifying glass, was the line along the binding where a razor blade or Exacto knife had made the little surgical cut.

Okay, there could be a lot of reasons for removing the page. A mistake in an inscription, a drop of coffee spilled on it, a sudden need for note paper with none in the house –

Yeah, and my dog ate the homework.

And now *he* had the moral dilemma. If he kept it from his wife, it would be the first time he had ever done such a thing. It was insignificant, men keep affairs and Swiss bank accounts and gambling addictions from their wives, so this?

But he knew it would become to him what the first Bible was to her, that little irritant that rubs like a grain of sand in your sock and won't stop, and every time he looked at this replacement Bible with that extracted page, and looked at her, he would be reminded —

On the other hand, if she did know, she would fret, and wonder whose Bible we have, maybe another Mrs. Peterson-and-her-daughter situation. Imagination can be an enemy as well as a friend, and this time there would be nothing to do about it, no Mount Roanoke to look up, just a mystery out there, nothing you could write to !READ! about –

The store that sold it.

No.

Utterly preposterous idea.

We have the store's name—the customer buys directly from the individual bookseller in the !Read! network—but books are commodities today, bought in bulk from estates, from publishers' overstocks, or from people in off the streets, cash transactions, and while the first thief was sloppy, this one was careful, razoring out the page, so how can you possibly go to a bookseller and ask if they know where they obtained this particular item?

Nobody who knew the book world would even think of it.

His wife would, though.

And then face the inevitable disappointment, inevitable.

Some little night creature scurried across the roof, the sound sliding up one side and down the other like a tiny laugh—just an illusion, he cautioned himself—but he remembered he was the one who had said *There's nothing you can do about it* and the one who had thought *!READ! will never answer* and the one who had said *They'll laugh at you* about the apartment all those years ago.

In the morning, he carried the Bible along with his coffee to the porch and said, "Let me show you something."

Furnished apartment available.

Low weekly rent.

No lease required.

Ideal for mature gentleman between commitments…

Friday, Daddy

What you'd expect for the price, Myron thought. Essentially one long room, maybe a parlor in the days when there were parlors, way before the old Victorian house had been chopped into these so-called apartments. A bed, a couch, a dresser, a table with two chairs, the basics, all with that picked-off-the-sidewalk look.

A two burner stove and mini refrigerator combination, a relic from some motel, filled a closet-sized alcove. The shelves above held the required few pots and pans. Myron found two tins of tuna inside one of the pots, evidently left by the previous tenant. A bonus, he said dryly, aware that he would use them. Every dollar counted now.

A door ajar next to the alcove showed a glimpse of the bathroom, which he didn't bother to inspect, simply making a bet with himself there would be a plunger next to the toilet.

He shrugged and flopped on the bed, calculating for the hundredth time. Mortgage payments, car payments, living expenses for Rita and Thelma, rent and food here, and no job. Damn Marlena and that scene in the office. Walking right in, screaming in front of the whole staff, his manager, was she nuts?

Probably, he conceded. He should have seen it from the beginning, the intensity, the willingness. But it was part of the attraction, wasn't it?

At least Marlena is one expense he would never have again. Along with the pleasures. It was certainly an adventure, he told the ceiling. He shifted on the bed, forcing his mind back to the calculations. The car payment could be delayed, the insurance, too, enough, maybe, to bring him through another month, two months if he borrowed from his brother. He made a gargling sound at the thought. But there would be a new job by then. There had to be. For all the joking about geeks and nerds, software engineers were in demand.

The divorce lawyers could be held off until then. They had enough experience to expect a delay. Thelma's sixth grade graduation was a different problem, though. A present—alright, he'd borrow from his brother, just for that. Attendance was the real worry. Going as a family would be a charade, a nerve wrenching one, but if he sat on the other side of the auditorium there would be the questions, the looks. When did sixth grade graduation become such a big deal?

World I never made, he sighed, knowing he did make it, at least that part of it that found him here on this sagging bed in a shabby room, his future home. I didn't need to snarl at Rita, he admitted. There was a chance she might be forgiving. Myron thought he had detected that. Trying to justify himself was where he went off the track, the attempt to explain men's needs, women's failure to adjust.

In this alien room, it sounded hollow. Marlena's hips, that little rolling motion, the way her eyes could widen, so blue, so innocent if you didn't know. He knew. There was never a moment when he didn't know. Most men are sexually arrested at fifteen, eternal adolescents, he read somewhere. Alright. Shouldn't Rita comprehend that? An educated woman, wasn't there a way to see his side? That there's a larger picture?

Somehow, "his side" was amorphous right now, a fog that he couldn't negotiate and he returned to calculating rent, utilities, the car, thinking he could skip lunches until he had an expense account again or saw a church fundraiser luncheon. They were always good, the donations small, the portions generous.

So that's how we get you back into church. He could hear Rita's voice. Not cynical, even a little amused, as always when she coaxed him. Soft spoken, stubborn, persistent. He had learned to deflect it, to smile agreeably, as if it were a game.

In truth, he could have gone with them on a Sunday now and then, an hour of tedium, no sacrifice really, a gesture for Rita, Thelma, too.

Careful. This must be what Langley, the lawyer, called the mea culpa factor. I see it over and over, Langley had warned him. Suddenly you're sorry, feel a touch of guilt and you know what happens? You start making concessions that you don't need to, that will bleed you the rest of your life.

But you see, Langley, it's my daughter I'm thinking about —

Give me a break, Langley had interrupted. Give me a chance to win for you. Nobody's going to starve. Your wife can go to work. No need to pamper her anymore. Every convenience store in town needs cashiers, the food packing company needs line workers. The ad's in the paper, she can read. The hospital needs kitchen staff, or maybe she has some college? He snapped his fingers in triumph at Myron's nod. Sub teaching then, always openings, good pay. See? Don't fall for the poverty bit, she'll get herself an income to help out. You don't need to shoulder it all.

He's right, Myron told himself with some vindictiveness now. I produced the income all these years, so let her have a taste of it, budgeting, managing. He began to calculate once more, his head squirming for a comfortable hollow in the lumpy pillow, his eyes closing.

He woke to darkness and voices. In his room? No, too metallic. A woman's voice and a man's. Good grief, would he have to listen to someone else's sexual encounter through the wall? No, walls were plaster and horsehair in these old houses, soundproof. The heating grate in the corner, then. Mrs. Rupp, the landlady, had proudly explained the old forced air system with its network of ducts and grates, the furnace originally wood fired, then coal, now natural gas, while showing him the ornamental little wrought iron panel in the floor.

He groped his way there in the dark, started to close it and the panel stuck. Forcing it would probably make the old metal hinges screech, revealing his presence, announcing that he might have been eavesdropping. He'd have to put something over it quietly, a pillow. There wouldn't be any heat in June.

"—you understand, Bobby, it's not one of those excusable divorces. This is a typical sordid affair and I want you to realize it."

The voice was Mrs. Rupp's. At least he didn't have to worry about unwanted carnal noises. Mrs. Rupp was in her seventies, easily, and used a four pronged cane to get around. But what was this about divorce?

"What the devil is an excusable divorce, Ma?" asked a male voice with a sarcastic edge to it. "Yours?"

"Mine, yes. No need to be snappy about it. Your father and I have both told you we were simply the wrong people, too different, too young when we married, both fooling ourselves. We tried. We stayed together far too many years. It became toxic, for us, for you."

"And your marriage vows? Before God? You could break those?"

Mrs. Rupp's voice dropped. "I will always wrestle with that. I will always pray for God's mercy, and with some justification. You will not be able to do that. A sordid affair, Bobby."

"Will you stop saying that?" Bobby's voice was sharp with anger. "How do you know my marriage wasn't toxic, as you call it? How do you know we weren't totally wrong for each other, just like you and Dad? That it came to a breaking point in the same way?"

"Bobby."

Just the one word, in the patient tone of a mother whose four-year-old has told a whopper.

"I'll go get some more coffee," Bobby said after a moment. Myron carefully sat down by the grate.

"At least allow that there were some cracks in our marriage," Bobby remarked when he returned. Cups clattered, the only response. "Alright, alright, I know what you want me to say. Every marriage has a few cracks and they're insignificant, you repair them and get on with life."

"Good," came the answer. "You've said it to me. Now say it to yourself and mean it."

"You want me to make a confession out of it. Next, I say it to God, right?"

"And much more. The affair, the pain you caused, the remorse, the redemption you want."

"Ma! Remorse? Redemption? I'm a twenty-first century guy getting a divorce. No big deal any more. Probably a dozen of us in this one street alone."

"And you think you can hide in the crowd? Cynthia will hurt less because there are others?"

"Ma, please."

"The kids?"

The Marble King and Other Stories

"Ma—"

"The responsibility is yours, Bobby. A dozen other men, a million other men, what does it matter? We're talking about Bobby Rupp. A solo act. Spotlight on you."

"And what do you expect me to do?" The sarcasm had disappeared. Bobby's voice was low and weary.

"Right now, you could pray. We could pray together. Remember?"

"Not that again, please." Bobby sighed. "Listen, it's late. Let's get some sleep."

"Yes, good. We'll talk some more tomorrow."

"About a sordid affair and remorse," Bobby said in resignation.

"At seventy-three, I say what I think. I love you, Bobby."

"I know, Ma."

"Also Cynthia and my grandchildren."

A grunt was the only response.

"And so do you, you darn fool kid," Mrs. Rupp said after the sound of a door closing. "Forty-four and still a darn fool kid."

I'm forty-four, thought Myron, finding the light switch, lifting a faded cushion from the couch to place over the grate in case Bobby returned. Enough talk for now.

Myron was almost giddy when he let himself in the next night. What a day, what a break! Last interview on the schedule, getting so tired of the forced smiles, the strained explanations of why he's out of work and bingo! a colleague from an earlier job is now the manager here, a genial guy, asks no personal questions (had a divorce of his own, Myron recalled), simply interested in results and knows how good Myron's work is, hired him on the spot, salary actually a few bucks more than the last job, offices bright and roomy and just a short bus ride from the apartment, a healthy walk, really, on sunny days.

A look around the room sobered him up a little—socks on the floor, underwear on the chair, shirt on the bed—this is where the healthy walk would bring him. Well, so what? It would bring him to independence. Couldn't a woman see how years of nagging about picking up this, picking up that, all the rest of it, would erode a man's affection, drive him to seek out some *understanding* elsewhere?

Well, he'd keep the place neat, on his own schedule. Fix it up a little, too, with some of his pictures from home—former home—the stadium shots would be good, and the photos of Thelma, especially the one where they were building a model of the USS Missouri. Was she seven then, that wonderfully loving age? Faces pinched in concentration, almost nose to nose, while he embedded the gun emplacements around the bridge. Rita had tiptoed in with her camera, giving them a photo moment that lasted, spoiling the actual moment with a comment about Daddy buying toys for himself, not really knowing what little girls like.

I like watching his fat fingers with the tiny ship thingees, Thelma had said. Myron laughed aloud now, as he had done back then, his arm encircling the air in a remembered hug. Rita couldn't leave it alone. Well, we need some toys for small fingers to handle, she said. Didn't even smile. Or did she? Myron tried to recollect the scene and gave it up. What's the difference? Just one more example of putting me down, ignoring my feelings.

He looked around the walls, weighing the best place to hang the photo, no, two photos. Next week would bring a graduation portrait. And he could buy that present now, no need to squeeze the money on hand—he blew a silent raspberry at his brother—and no need for those leftover tuna cans. He stopped himself as he opened the cupboard door. A celebration tonight, a restaurant meal and then shopping, an Ipad mini probably. With a pink case. How Thelma would squeal with joy. Let Rita try to object.

Myron did a little two step into the room when he returned, still tasting the prime rib dinner, holding the showily wrapped gift in his arms like a dance partner. I'm light on my feet for my size, he informed the package. He blew it a kiss, bowed, placed it with care on the dresser and started to tidy up, two stepping all the while. Swooping down to retrieve a sock, he heard a voice below, faint beneath the cushion.

He continued around the room, his curiosity held in check for a few seconds. As the voice rose—it was Bobby's—he shrugged and pushed the cushion aside.

"—the small things, Ma, you don't understand, the small things, how they add up."

"I understand how they can be exaggerated if you want."

"If I want? You're insulting me now."

"Of course. You earned it. A whip for the horse, a bridle for the ass, and a rod for the fool's back."

"Now don't throw Proverbs at me."

"Good, you remember the source."

"Yes, I still know Scripture, and I know Solomon said it, and do you think any of his wives told him to change the furnace filter and gave him that look? The one you're giving me right now?"

"The furnace filter? A 30-second chore? Lift out the old one, slip in the new one? That's cause to run off with some floozie?"

Bobby's voice grew high pitched with resentment. "Not the chore, the look! Head to one side, little superior smile."

Upstairs, Myron nodded. With Rita, it was shoulders hunched, a finger lifted, but the same little superior smile; he could picture it clearly.

"Yes, I've seen it on Cynthia. Bobby, it's affectionate."

"Ma, it's degrading, and it's not just the furnace filter, it's mow the lawn, patch the screen door, the shutter's loose upstairs, did you buy new faucet washers? You'll tell me all that stuff is part of life and it is, and I do get around to doing it all, but it's her attitude, her constant reminding. Did you know both boys laugh at me? Daddy forgot again, ha, ha."

"And they laughed at Mommy for pushing her shopping cart into a cereal display. I was there. But if you're worrying about keeping their respect, you'll certainly keep it by abandoning them."

Overhead, Myron visibly winced.

"You're telling yourself fairy tales, deliberately," she continued. "What I said before, exaggerating all the small things because you want to. What about at night?"

"What?"

"At night, at night, you know what I mean."

"I won't talk about *that* with you."

"So it was all right, then. Any problems were from your insensitivity, not hers. Don't argue, I can read your face. I've been doing it since you took your first breath."

"Look, I didn't bring that subject up. I'm talking about—"

"I know, furnace filters. And maybe you'll tell me about the times you're ready to go somewhere and she won't get off the phone. Or you go to the mall to get coats for the kids and she drags you to housewares and curtains and bedding and whatnot first. Does she put her hair spray in the bathroom cabinet so you can't reach your after shave? Or the pork and beans you like— sometimes there's not a can in the house, right? And she gives you that look when your football game runs overtime? Am I on the right track? A bunch of terrible things like that?"

Bobby's voice rose again. "Make fun all you want, a can of beans, hair spray, but it shows a lack of regard for me and it adds up. It's the accumulation, day in, day out, the accumulation!"

Myron's head shake of agreement was stopped short by a small crash below.

"Ma? What are you doing? You can't stand without the cane."

"Thirty years of rheumatoid arthritis, Bobby. I know about day in, day out. Pain in every joint. Standing, sitting, lying down." She stopped for a deep, rasping breath. Then, in a voice that penetrated as if there were no grate, no floor between, "That's an accumulation, Bobby. You don't have an accumulation. You know what you have?"

"Ma, please sit down."

"An alibi!"

Silence followed. It lasted so long, Myron checked his watch. Five minutes already. He laid down on the floor, his ear to the grate to make sure he wasn't missing anything.

Finally, Bobby said, "I'll get your cane." He was restrained now. So was his mother.

"Yes. Come to the kitchen. Some warm milk? It always helped you sleep."

"I remember. You, too, Ma."

Myron woke from a restless night, fragments of a dream chasing around: trying on a jacket for graduation, the tailor having Langley's face, then Thelma's voice through the grate, *Friday, Daddy,* and he was in the auditorium, all the men in identical jackets, could he push through without crushing the bow on the IPad Mini, push through, keep pushing, but to where? He sat up, pawing at the air, *Friday, Daddy,* still sounding.

In the office, he caught himself staring at the calendar so often he finally turned it around. After work, he indulged in another restaurant dinner, finding he had to remind himself from time to time he was enjoying it. At a nearby table, an attractive and smartly dressed brunette glanced at him, then held the glance deliberately. Myron looked away, while accepting the compliment with no surprise. He was no movie star, he knew that, and yes, he was even a bit, well, portly, yet he carried himself easily and had in his face a boyishness—Rita's word, in better times—that always seemed to intrigue certain women. Idly, he pictured himself walking out with the brunette. Good looking couple, people would think. They would do the same, he recognized, if it were Rita on his arm.

Raindrops began outside the restaurant, gathering into a steady fall by the time Myron reached the house, blurring lights and hushing street noises, a hush that continued inside. It was cool, tranquil and Myron welcomed it. He changed clothes and lay down by the grate without even thinking, dozing until the voices began, soft tonight, like the rain.

The talk was of relatives, a catalogue of uncles and aunts and nephews and nieces, their successes, failures, eccentricities (Uncle Herman and his sword collection brought a laugh, a little too extended, and Myron understood they were intentionally avoiding *the* subject); they reminisced about vacations, the Wichita Fair, Pikes Peak, the bike bridge across the Des Moines River, thirteen stories high; discussed the neighborhood, the old stores gone, over-elegant boutiques in their place, a Starbucks on their own corner, imagine... finally, Mrs. Rupp brought the conversation around.

"Boredom, Bobby."

Bobby tried to fend it off. "You've never been in a Starbucks. The prices are beyond—"

"That's really what we were talking about last night," she pushed on. "Boredom. Sixteen years of marriage, an affliction sets in and it leads you to—you don't like sordid affair. What do I call it?" She continued without waiting for an answer. "Boredom is like a disease with no immune system to protect you."

The Marble King and Other Stories

"I know where you're heading with this, Ma. You expect me to pick up a Bible, or pray, and poof! an immune system."

"No, not poof! You've been away from it too long. But a start, Bobby, a start. Tomorrow—" She trailed off.

"Tomorrow, I know. I walk into the lawyer's office and I sign separation papers."

"Or?"

"Or I call Cynthia first and ask if we can get back together. I don't know that I want to do it and you can't assure me that she'll say yes."

"Nobody can. I think she will, though, and I know that if I pray and you pray, we'll be heard."

"We'll be heard," Bobby repeated flatly.

"Don't dismiss it that way. You're churning inside and I see it. Who knows you better than I do? Churning inside. I want some relief for you." The old lady's steady voice was breaking for the first time.

"Please don't, Ma. I'm an adult, I'm responsible for myself. I never should have come here. When you come home you're always nine years old again."

"Oh! The poem," she cut in abruptly. "You reminded me. Bobby, the poem."

"What? You mean Longfellow? Ma, that's a prayer. You're forcing me."

"Then forget I'm trying to help you. Do it for me. You used to read it so beautifully. Remember the church recitals?"

"Thirty-five years ago. Let's not—"

"It's in the bookcase where we always kept it. Collected Poems."

"Yes, yes. The green cover. But Ma, please. "

The old lady said nothing, yet whatever was exchanged in the looks between them brought the sound of footsteps leaving, returning, and then Bobby's voice, reciting:

144

"Let us then labor for an inward stillness - "

"No, wait." He cleared his throat several times, then began again in a surprisingly pleasant baritone, light but perfectly modulated.

"Let us then labor for an inward stillness -
An inward stillness and an inward healing;

The baritone grew richer now, deeper.

"That perfect silence where the lips and the heart
Are still, and we no longer entertain
Our own imperfect thoughts and vain opinions,

Here he slowed, making each phrase slow and measured.

"But God alone speaks in us, and we wait
In singleness of heart, that we may know
His will, and in the silence of our spirits,
That we may do His will, and do that only."

The final words fell into a stillness of their own, leaving only rain to be heard.

Rita would love that poem, thought Myron. He would Google it tonight, print it out, Longfellow, let us labor for an inward stillness, easy enough to remember, give it to her at graduation. If they sat together. Mail it otherwise, a token of—something.

Mrs. Rupp's voice came at last.

"You feel better now, different and better."

"Ma, there are no miracle solutions here."

"Bobby. This is me you're talking to."

"A little better, then. Alright, more than a little. But Ma, be realistic, my choice for tomorrow is no closer."

"Alright. Should we try some warm milk again? And Bobby, did you ever notice that it's always the other person who's not being realistic?"

Myron woke from another dream in the morning, a dream of talking to Bobby Rupp in a rainstorm that blotted out faces, tactfully trying to explain to Bobby how he knew so much about him and trying to worm out of him his decision for today.

At his office computer, Myron started to work, suspended it after a few minutes and typed Robert Rupp into the browser. Robert A. Rupp, the screen told him, teacher of high school mathematics, author of the widely used textbook, *Algebra Basics.*

So that was Bobby's daytime world, numbers and symbols, the cold logic of equations, the interplay of assigned values. If anybody could solve a problem, it would be math teacher Rupp. And if anybody could be paralyzed by a problem it would be math teacher Rupp. In today's example, class, can anyone here assign algebraic values to a wife, a mistress and two children? Oh, and a furnace filter?

Not funny, Myron, he told himself. We're a pair of eggheads, a mathematician and a computer nerd, trying to navigate a landscape of the heart, not the brain. No signposts. MapQuest doesn't go here. You and the lawyer's meeting today, me and the graduation tomorrow. Do you sign the papers or call your Cynthia? Do I sit apart or ask to sit with Rita, and there's a symbol for you, Daddy and Mommy side by side, the erring husband returning, seeking remorse and redemption as your mother puts it. Do I honestly want it? Your crummy room is a symbol, too, freedom, living my own schedule. So, teacher Rupp, I'm really curious about your choice and your Cynthia's response. Okay, more than really curious. Let's say eager. You're not praying, are you? The way you read that poem last night…

Myron walked directly home after work, moving briskly, taking no time for a restaurant, stopping instead at a convenience store to buy bread, mayonnaise and milk, tapping his foot impatiently at the checkout counter.

His eyes went right to the grate when he entered the apartment, aware it was too early, unable to curb the reflex. He put together a rapid supper of the abandoned tuna and his grocery items and ate sitting by the grate. Gazing around the room, he was momentarily surprised by its neatness, then remembered he had picked up his things the previous night.

The voices came and Myron frowned. They were too distant to be heard clearly. He waited for them to come nearer. When they didn't, he leaned down and pressed his ear tight against the metal. No improvement. Bobby and his mother were in some far corner of the room where their words could not be made out.

Tonight? he whispered at them? You had to sit somewhere else tonight? He stood up and walked softly into the hall outside, seeking another grate that might be closer. He found none. Back in the room, he resumed his place, straining to hear a word or two, or to catch the mood, but only a murmuring came through. He stayed for a while after the voices ceased, just in case they returned, then yielded and went to bed.

Sometime in the night, frustrated and sleepless, Myron turned on his laptop. Maybe some TV reruns—the poem was still there from last night. He read slowly, not fully focused, silent until the line, 'God alone speaks in us.' He uttered that aloud, only vaguely aware he was doing so. "God alone speaks in us," he repeated and continued, "and we wait in singleness of heart, that we may know His will."

Myron tapped the screen, conscious now that he was talking. "That's the point, God, singleness of heart. I've got a confusion of heart here, with no enlightenment from the math teacher downstairs, and I don't know what your will is."

He paused and considered his tone of voice. "I'm irritable, God. If I'm praying, irritable is a dumb way to go. Am I praying? Look, I apologize. I mean, I'm not proud of myself. I'm actu-

The Marble King and Other Stories

ally remorseful about everything that's happened. Repentance, that's the word, isn't it? Sinners, repent, and I'm a sinner." Myron grimaced at the words. "God, I'm not comfortable with this. Sounds like pulpit talk, always about guilt. I need time to think, amen." He stumbled back to bed.

He woke at daybreak, irritability outweighed by anxiety. This was Friday. *Friday, Daddy.* The anxiety grew, cramping his back and neck muscles on the walk to work. He stopped for breakfast, ordering coffee and toast without hearing himself, eating without tasting anything.

At the computer, he heard a voice behind him, felt a tap on the shoulder. "A little day dreaming on company time, Myron?" The voice was friendly, a co-worker passing by, teasing him about his screen. Column after column of Friday, Daddy filled the space.

Myron took a long breath, exhaled slowly, reached for the phone.

"Rita? It's Myron."

"Yes?" It was guarded.

"Will you, can you, save a seat for me at graduation?"

A pause, then, "Yes."

"I mean next to you, sitting together."

"I knew what you meant."

"And, uh, I was thinking we could take Thelma for some ice cream after."

"She's been invited to a party."

"Oh." Myron steeled himself, then said, "Well, maybe we could go, just the two of us."

Myron heard Rita take a long breath of her own.

"It's supposed to be warm and humid," she said.

"You mean a good night for ice cream?"

"If you'd like."

Mrs. Rupp and Bobby watched the taxi until it turned the corner past Starbucks, out of sight.

"This was a quick one," Bobby said. "Think it's the new script?"

"Maybe. The alibi line is dramatic. Cuts right to the lies they tell themselves. You're not a bad playwright for a math teacher."

"And you're a decent actress for a math teacher's mother. But I'm still not sure of that last part, where we move to the corner of the room and my choice, my supposed choice, can't be heard."

"Trust me, you've got it right. They need to be keyed up toward a decision, but not get a push from what they think you did. They have to find it themselves and even better, see that it's God's hand."

"I wonder if he did." Bobby pointed in the taxi's direction.

"I wouldn't be surprised. You gave your best performance yet with the poem."

"Well, Longfellow. There's a script writer for you. Listen, I think I better go now. The kids have Little League and if I miss it again, Cynthia may send *me* to that room upstairs. By the way, is it shabby enough or should I make another flea market trip?"

"No need. It's depressing enough to make any man think of home."

"Okay, then. Are you ready for another try? Shall I put the listing in?"

"Yes, and don't get creative. It's just fine as it as."

"I know. It's uncanny how it always brings in the right man. 'Furnished apartment available. Low weekly rent No lease required. Ideal for mature gentleman between commitments.'" Bobby chuckled. "You're sure I can't add Free Theatre! Original Script! Superb Cast!"

"Go on home, Bobby," she said.

149

"It's one of those things about war that's hard to understand. People are being blown up and starving and dying while others benefit…"

Brownstone 1942

"Catch your breath," Mrs. Gemiani told me. My writing is what she was talking about. She stood at my desk, my newest composition in one hand, the index finger of her other hand circling under my nose, not the menace it may sound like because Mrs. Gemiani is understanding and young enough to wear high heels. The circling finger actually focused your mind so you paid attention, although when I tried that on my dad in a discussion about comic books, he quietly folded my finger down and placed my hand on the table. (Mom would have batted the finger away) (Not hard, just a stop-the-nonsense bat.)

"Slow down, Janine," Mrs. Gemiani was saying. "Choose one theme and stay on a direct path, a step at a time, instead of all the byroads." She shook my paper. The fourteen pages rustled nicely. "Now this is about moving to Brooklyn. Unless it's about the war. Or your parents. Or your sister. Or your pen pal in the navy. Or Rhoda Stern (my best friend, who I won't see any more because

The Marble King and Other Stories

of the move). Or living in a brownstone in Chelsea. You see the problem? The reader must have one central theme to follow. I've marked this 'A' because you write so remarkably well for your age but next time you must pick a path and follow it, one crisp sentence at a time, one crisp paragraph at a time, step, step, step." She went back to her desk, sort of marching up the aisle so her high heels went step, step, step, to demonstrate, I guess.

I wanted to please her. I couldn't quite see how to do what she wanted, though. Let's take writing about the move. Right at this minute there are corrugated boxes on the floor where our winter clothes and photo albums and good china dishes and such are piling up and I don't really want to think about it, but I'll go ahead and write about it. My neighbor, Mr. Gramley, said writing helps you come to terms with unpleasant things and I believed him but immediately I wondered if he wrote about having this illness, diabetes, which keeps him from the army. He took classes and became our Air Raid Warden and Emergency Medical Aide but I know he's not satisfied with those things when men his age are away fighting and, well, there you are: I mention Mr. Gramley and a story about moving to Brooklyn gets off the path to be about the war, not to mention that the war changed my dad's job, making us move.

He's the machinery maven, expert, at a millinery factory. He keeps everything running. The factory is on Seventh Avenue, about twelve blocks from our brownstone. My dad usually walks to work. But the factory is now getting government contracts to make hats for soldiers and sailors and pilots and marines instead of hats for ladies.

It's one of those things about war that's hard to understand. People are being blown up and starving and dying while others benefit. My dad's factory will be making half a million hats this year instead of fifty thousand, he says, but they can't do it on Seventh Avenue. They need a huge building and there's one in Brooklyn that's just right, and where they'll make so much money my dad will have two assistants and his salary will be more than doubled!

The thing about the new factory is that it's not in nearby Brooklyn across the bridge. It's in faraway Brooklyn along the ocean, an hour-and-a-half by subway and bus, so we need to live out there.

Dad told Mom and me he's uneasy about all that money, even a little guilty. Mom said nobody would be helped by his turning it down and we could donate more money to whatever church we went to in Brooklyn and buy War Bonds and do other good things.

I suggested two comic books a week instead of one and laughed along with them. (The idea was now subtly planted.)

My comic books come from Meyerson's Candy and Magazines across the street, where I go every day to get my dad his newspaper, and even that's part of the war because each time I go through the door, the sound of Mr. Meyerson's radio is lurking in my head, I mean the sound on that particular Sunday when I was choosing my weekly comic book and sipping an ice cold chocolate milk, really *ice* cold because they keep the milk containers in this bin full of frozen chips and they keep the glasses in a refrigerator. Mrs. Meyerson can barely hold one when she mixes in the syrup. Your teeth hurt and your ears jingle after a few sips, it's so deliciously, chocolaty cold and so I missed whatever Mr. Meyerson was calling to Mrs. Meyerson until he turned up the little radio by the cash register where he listens to the football game and then it came through, Pearl Harbor and everything.

I knew the name. Most people never heard of it, but almost two years ago, a sailor from the USS Helena flirted with my big sister, Madeleine, at the piers when the Queen Mary, the Queen

Elizabeth and the Normandy, the world's three biggest liners, all docked together and the USS Helena was there, too, picking up supplies on the way to Pearl Harbor.

When we heard thirty-four sailors on his ship were killed, we wondered. Our whole family had been on the pier and liked him. His forwardness with Madeleine was just having fun, you could tell. "We never found out his name," my dad said, "what can we do?" I didn't say anything but wrote a letter and addressed the envelope to USS Helena, Pacific Fleet (To The Sailor Who Flirted With A Beautiful Brunette On The Chelsea Piers, March 14, 1940).

I told him Madeleine was married now and I was the small, sort of round girl with the spiky, straw-colored hair holding her hand, although I'm lengthening somewhat now that I'm eleven. My family hoped he was OK.

Two months after, we got a letter. His name was Jimmy Denison, he was okay and the whole ship was kidding him about the envelope address. He said he was really flirting with me that day, not Madeleine (he's funny!) and he'd appreciate mail, so he's the pen pal Mrs. Gemiani mentioned. Madeleine said he'll never know what hit him, about letters from me. She doesn't know I'm improving.

Getting back to that Meyerson's day, when I rushed home to tell Mom and Dad, they already knew and so did the whole brownstone. People were gathering outside their apartments, sitting on the stairs, talking in that soft way they do if somebody is sick although you could hear they were angry and I heard the word "Japs" with some bad language and got a little nervous about this really nice boy, Joey Matsuhara, who was in my grade then, although he's gone now. He was completely American and played stickball and everything and couldn't possibly like the idea of sinking our ships. To him, they'd be his ships, too.

Mrs. Gemiani shuffled everybody around so there's no empty space where he used to sit, although maybe she should have left it as a reminder for those who said mean things to Joey and slipped horrible notes in his book bag. They all say they're sorry now. When Mrs. Gemiani gave us a lecture on tolerance, none of them could look at her.

Nobody knew where the Matsuharas went. The rumor was Mr. Matsuhara got fired from his job and they left for the West Coast, where Japanese, I mean American Japanese, are being kept in what they call internment camps, like army barracks. They felt a camp was better than the insults here, the rumor goes.

Rhoda was looking down at her desk and biting her lip like she does when she's upset during Mrs. Gemiani's lecture, which surprised me because she and I were always part of the crowd of kids who were Joey's friends—but I'm on a byroad here.

Direct path, Janine, so I'll go back again to sitting on the stairs with the neighbors on Pearl Harbor Day, and I became scared for all of us in the brownstone when I heard Mr. Stokes, the quiet bald man with a cane who lived in 1A, say to someone, "No, no, there's no way they can bomb New York City. California, maybe, not here." Is it possible we should even have to think about that? I imagined the brownstone collapsing, bathtubs and ceiling beams and people falling through floors, us, the Bogulubovs across the hall, the Macilenneys upstairs.

That night, I listened and could just about hear rumbles and booms coming closer and Mom somehow knew and came in and said she heard them, too, and explained it was the ordinary truck and 23rd Street subway station noises, made spooky, she said, by our fears. I asked what Dad thought and she said, "Who knows? He's snoring," and that made things normal and I fell asleep.

The Marble King and Other Stories

We had blackouts and dim-outs and air raid drills after that Sunday but the fear of bombs in Chelsea went away and the war became something that was just *here*, like at Meyerson's, or when I pass by Shop class in school and the boys are making those airplane models for the air force so pilots can identify enemy planes from friendly ones, or Home Ec, where I'm trying to knit socks without lumps in them for displaced families, or collecting tin cans for the scrap metal drives, or when Madeleine calls and the first thing we ask is whether Mike, my brother-in-law, will have to go to England. They're in Boston, where he has what they call an essential job, an engineer in a factory where they make machine gun parts for English planes and there's talk he's needed at that end to make sure they're installed right. Madeleine's going to have a baby and she's a little frantic. I would be, too.

It's not that we're depressed, I mean my friends and I (except about the move). The resiliency of youth, my dad says, and I still get comic books and chocolate milk at Meyerson's, and I still take these long walks with Rhoda through Chelsea and it's the world's greatest show, the brownstones lined up, sort of on parade, and the small apartment houses they call tenements although they're all scrubbed clean with flowerpots on every fire escape, and all the shops—there's this one place where you can buy jade jewelry and get your pants pressed, if you're a man, right in the same narrow little shop, and a really wrinkled Chinese lady sits on a wooden bench outside sometimes, just staring, and there's this antique shop, Chelsea Past, selling huge, dark dressers with dusty mirrors and old bookcases still filled with their old books and the owner lets us wander through and make up stories about them while he plays the violin for us, truly! He's tall and thin and wears a beret and Rhoda, who's been studying piano for years, says he's playing Debussy and Dvorak and he's really good. (I'll never find this in Brooklyn!)

BROWNSTONE 1942

Also there's Moscowitz Brothers Kosher Delicatessen where the pickle smell can knock you down. We're handed a slice of rye bread with mustard from Rhoda's Uncle Bernie or Uncle Kenny every time we stop in and it may not sound too appetizing but it's actually delicious. It even started me writing a poem that took two nights and a lot of really hard concentrating to get just right.

Hold forever the tang
Of mustard on your tongue
As you step into the sun
Of an April Chelsea day
Clotheslines gaily hung
Baby carriages abounce
On hopscotch-chalked sidewalks
Gauzy window curtains
Hide busy family secrets.
Debussy, pickles, jade, uncles,
A friend.
Hold it all. Tight. Forever.

Mrs. Gemiani looked astonished and asked, "Janine, did you really write this?" and I felt tears coming right there in class, it was such a hurtful question, and she thought and said, "I'm sorry, dear, yes, this sort of writing is well within your grasp now." She thought again and said, "You're breaking through."

Mr. Gramley, whose real job is Associate Professor of History at City College, not Air Raid Warden, and who's known me for years and encourages me to write, said, "Ah, a brownstone farewell poem. Beautiful, and very helpful. I see a touch of Shelley, a touch of Robert Frost, exactly right. You know, poetry like

157

this means you're capable of adult, even professional level prose. Carry on."

I showed the poem to Mom and Dad after thinking it over. I didn't want it to look like a complaint. They said it was beautiful and they understood.

For dinner that night, Mom made zurcher geschnetzeltes, veal and mushrooms and cream sauce (we're Swiss by ancestry, here for three generations but the old food names stick), an absolute favorite of mine. Then after dinner, she gave me money to go to Macy's the next day, the first day of our Easter break from school, so I could buy new church shoes, the black patent leather kind, with silvery or gold buckles.

I said, "Me? Myself?" This had never happened before.

"You, yourself. Rhoda, too, if you want. Make sure they fit."

I knew I would. Church shoes matter because we go to the Chapel of the Good Shepherd on 21st Street, with its huge stained glass windows and statues and everything polished and glowing. I know it doesn't make you any more faithful but somehow you feel better in patent leather and a starched dress and we go every week now, not just on Christmas and Easter. All the families in the brownstone do, since Pearl Harbor. The building empties like a subway exit on Sunday morning.

Rhoda's family goes every week now, too, on Saturday morning, to a synagogue down the street near Tenth Avenue. They come home walking slowly, sadly, and despite what Mrs. Gemiani expects, I have to take a byroad here to explain why.

One day at Moscowitz Brothers, Rhoda's Uncle Bernie handed us the rye bread and mustard without really seeing us, looking grim, and Uncle Kenny was talking very low to a customer and they were both patting at their eyes.

Rhoda found her parents the same way when she got home and she had to nag at them to get an answer and finally they told her the Moscowitzes had learned that first cousins of theirs in Poland had died at Belzec, a concentration camp, and that *all* Jewish families were being taken away to the camps and would be gassed to death.

Since the Moscowitzes were relatives of the Sterns, their cousins would be Rhoda's cousins in some way and there were certainly lots of other, unknown Stern family members whose grandparents never left Poland and their descendants, even little children, tiny cousins she didn't know but they were connected, were now gone or suffering terribly.

There were so many other people in the synagogue in the same situation, exchanging horrifying news with each other, and praying in tears, you could understand why they walked home so grim.

It was also clear why Rhoda looked down and bit her lip at Mrs. Gemiani's lecture about Joey Matsuhara, and condemning an entire people. Internment camps made her think of concentration camps and while we know they're not the same, and we're never going to have gas chambers, Rhoda said her dad said, "Our people are born with this fear deep inside, so many centuries."

I felt separated from her for a strange moment, and then closer than ever and we hugged tight and I told her, "Call me all the time in Brooklyn, whenever you feel unhappy, especially."

On the Macy's shopping day, Dad slipped some money into my hand as I left. "Lunch for you and Rhoda at the Automat," he said.

This was better than an extra comic book. The Automat is where they stow the food in cubbyholes with glass doors which open when you inject a nickel and then reach in for history's best-ever baked beans in a little brown crock, or an American cheese-with-lettuce sandwich or a chocolate pudding, or all of them, actually. I like food, which is why I'm a little round. Mom says not to worry about it; I'll be a blond version of Madeleine in a few years. With all those boys hanging around? Maybe I'll like it by then.

Rhoda and I skipped along the ten blocks to Macy's more than we walked. Shopping alone! No parents! We decided to go to Girl's Shoes first, so I'd have a Macy's bag to carry around, making it clear we were real shoppers, not sight-seeing kids.

A skinny young salesman, more of a salesboy, a high school part-timer, I guessed, hired because so many men were at war, measured my feet and brought over a small cart of shoes. He whistled 'Chattanooga Choo Choo' at the ceiling while I tried on every pair and then picked a pair with silver buckles, not for the buckles but for the bit of a heel, maybe half-an-inch, enough to make me feel tall and daring. The salesboy whistled 'Chattanooga Choo Choo' at me, not the ceiling, when I walked a circle in them and he waggled his eyebrows, laughing when I turned a little red.

We strolled through the rest of the third floor, Women's Apparel, pushing each other at some of the Intimate Garments, then took the escalator to Furniture, trying the armchairs and sofas, and flopping on mattresses, where a stout woman with a supervisor's badge pointed us to the exit, and we rode up to Five: Toys, Books and Musical Instruments. We admired the dolls and doll houses until Rhoda asked if this wasn't beneath someone with heels on her shoes, so we pushed each other some more and went to Musical Instruments, rows of pianos on the floor and violins and guitars and trumpets and such on the walls, all fenced in by a polished wooden railing.

Rhoda went directly to a Steinway grand piano and stood licking her lips. I'm sure she didn't know she was doing it. Her home piano was a small, scratched upright. She gulped, looked at me as if for approval and I said, "They're here to be tried out."

BROWNSTONE 1942

She sat and played a few notes and said, "ooh" at the rolling sound. Then she plunged right into a piece I recognized as Chopin because I'd heard it at her home. A couple of salesmen came over, and then some customers one by one, so that she had an audience and they all applauded when she finished and one of the salesmen shouted, "Brava!"

Rhoda glowed, I mean just lit up and when we left she held on to me as if she needed an anchor to keep from floating away.

She was still giddy when we reached Books, humming Chopin while I looked over the best-seller display, where Frenchman's Creek by Daphne du Maurier was propped on the counter. I traced my finger over Daphne du Maurier and Rhoda said, "I'm going to ask the saleswomen for the latest best-seller by Janine Sarni."

"No, you won't," I said. "Come down to earth."

"Yes, I will," she answered and actually started toward the desk with a serious look but halfway there she turned around and she couldn't hold the expression and she giggled. So did I, and then we had a giggling fit that neither of us could control and we rode the escalator down and up and down again, giggling our way through all five of Macy's floors, until we were outside in Herald Square and we took some deep, deep breaths and went down 34th Street to the Automat and ate without talking and then walked home silently, arm in arm, knowing this was the last time, except when we reached her brownstone she began to whistle 'Chattanooga Choo Choo" and we broke out giggling again.

The following Saturday was my first Brooklyn trip

Mom and Dad had been there three times on days when I was in school and they found an apartment in a neighborhood called Marine Park and I think I have to do something now: switch to third person like a story about someone else so I can keep control of it.

161

Here:

The bus pulls to the curb. Janine peeks again at her father's watch. It's been a dreary hour and three minutes on the subway and thirty-two more minutes on this bus. "Last stop," the driver calls. Janine closes the Dixie Dugan comic she's read three times during the trip.

She has not yet seen the house she will live in. It's only two years old, her mom had told her (Janine is leaving behind a wonderfully lived-in brownstone of sixty-five years). A new kitchen, her mom said, a new refrigerator, new stove and a linoleum floor, so easy to clean. Her dad's happy there's natural gas for heat, the most efficient system you can get. No more rattling coal trucks, he said, or coal falling off the chute or all that black stuff fouling the air. He sure won't miss any of it.

Janine doesn't tell him she will, at least the trucks like giant toys and the grumpy automobile drivers stuck behind the delivery and the way the coal swooshes like an avalanche down the chute into the basement, part of a show she'll never see in Marine Park.

There is one promising sight, though, a storefront by the bus stop, Tully's Periodicals and Tobacco, with a newspaper rack out on the sidewalk and a window sign for MelloRol Ice Cream Cones. This looks like the place to pick up her dad's newspaper, and treats for herself, if Tully's is close to their destination—and it is. A block away, two-story row houses line the street. Row houses are related to brownstones in some ways. They're attached, they have differently painted doors so the tired family member returning from work or school will enter the right home, and they have front stoops like brownstones, although too wide and too short (five steps compared to a brownstone's thirteen) to be truly authentic.

They stop at a house with a dark green door. There are two apartments per house and hers is the one upstairs. Her dad and mom eagerly take her through the rooms, six of them—living room, dining room, kitchen, three bedrooms—both parents talking at once, concerned that she like everything, pointing at room size and sunlight and air and the view (other houses, fewer people, more sky than Chelsea) and she obediently agrees how nice it is.

They leave the apartment for a short walk to the east, to Marine Park—a real park that gives the neighborhood its name—more than one thousand acres, her dad announces, far bigger than Central Park, with canoeing, camping, hiking and bird watching.

To the south, another short walk away, her dad says, is a beach and a bay where they can sunbathe and haul up clams, oysters and crabs. Janine makes a small gagging sound, unheard. Or they can get on a fishing boat for mackerel, striped bass, porgies and fluke, even bluefish and tuna if it's a deep sea boat. She tries to picture her dad from the streets of Chelsea landing a tuna, or canoeing, camping, hiking and bird watching. She coughs politely.

Her mom wants one more look at the new kitchen, so they return to the house. On the stoop across the street, a girl who appears the same age as Janine sits reading a comic book. She has short, shiny black hair with a large orange ribbon. The comic book cover seems to be one of the new Archie series. Janine holds up her Dixie Dugan comic. The black-haired girl moves her head from side to side, a "so what," opinion of Dixie Dugan, but she crosses the street anyway.

She's Rose Marie Rienza and she might be interested in comic book trading. Archie, Disney and Captain Tootsie are her favorites, which Janine finds a little icky although Rose Marie does like Wonder Woman, giving them some common interest to build on. Rose Marie will also introduce her to everybody at school. Janine had been pushing away the thought of being The New Girl.

She thanks Rose Marie and asks if the sixth grade teacher gives a lot of writing assignments. Rose Marie says Yes, all the time, and she talks and talks about writers and writing, drives you nuts. Janine brightens.

She brightens again, excitedly, upstairs. When she asks idly what they'll do with the third bedroom, her mom says it's for Madeleine and the baby. What? You heard something? Mike is going to England?

They haven't actually heard, but Dad, who understands anything to do with machinery, says it has to happen, and soon. He starts to explain about tolerances and fittings and precision grinding, and how that requires the engineer who designed the fittings to be there at the assembly point. She puts on her admiring smile for Dad, while she imagines holding a niece or nephew (Aunt Janine!) and wheeling him or her around in a carriage, and being with Madeleine was always fun...

Alright, I've lost it, I mean third person. This is me writing again, feeling childish, guilty, really, for being excited about Madeleine and a baby in the next room without thinking first of Mike and Madeleine being separated, and how miserable that will make them. But otherwise, I think I've told about Brooklyn maturely, no lamenting.

There will be a truck from Dad's factory and men from the shipping and packing section to help move because real moving companies are so hard to get in wartime. The factory owner is giving us his car and driver for the day to take Mom and Dad and me and the small, breakable vases and Hummel figurines and such that Mom won't trust to a truck. So Sunday will be my last day in our brownstone.

Sunday is tomorrow.

BROWNSTONE 1942

It's two days later, Monday, and I'm writing in my new room. From the window, I can see Rose Marie Rienza and two other girls sitting on the stoop and talking and looking up here now and then. They look okay, I mean no giggling behind their hands, no heads together whispering, just talking. I could go over and bring some comic books—Dad gave me money for five of them this afternoon! Mom is taking me to register at school tomorrow and the more friends I already have there the less I'll seem like The New Girl. I know all that. Still, barging into a strange group...I'll try to work up to it.

Yesterday when we came home from church, the Bogulubovs brought a cake with God Bless You, Sarni Family spelled out in blue icing, and other neighbors came in and out all afternoon to tell us how much we'd be missed, and it was a teary time for the women and a lot of handshaking and back-slapping for the men and head patting for me, until Rhoda came and we went to my room for a grown-up goodbye, no weeping, just a lot of laughing at the silliest of the times we had, and promising to phone and write, and agreeing it was good that she would be in school Monday when I drove off. Actually seeing it could be painful.

It was eight o'clock before everything quieted down and we were alone, the three of us. Mom and Dad were wandering around, staring at the furniture, touching a table or a chair, re-checking everything that was to be moved, I thought, and I started for my room to write some more and it hit me: they weren't re-checking things, they were remembering things.

You dolt, Janine. You selfish dolt. How could you not realize this move could be as hard for them as for you. Harder. You've lived here eleven years, they've lived here twenty-three, all the years of their marriage, their only home...

The Marble King and Other Stories

"The new apartment's really great," I said. "All that space, and light, and the park, and I think Rose Marie and I will be terrific friends."

They looked at me as if I were speaking Greek, then Dad said, "You're a poor liar but a wonderfully brave little girl."

"Young lady," Mom corrected.

"Brave young lady," Dad agreed, and we sat on the sofa for a long while after that, me in the middle, the two of them leaning over me like a tent, Mom playing with this spiky hair of mine and the truth is, I felt like a little girl again and it was nice (although I won't let it become a habit). We talked some about how Dad might be able to come home for lunch, the new factory being so close, and about buying fresh fish at the bay, and fixing up the room for Madeleine and the baby, things like that, but mostly just sitting quietly until Mom said, "We need some music," so I brought in the Decca portable Madeleine had left me and some of her records, Glenn Miller and the Andrews Sisters and Frank Sinatra and Kay Kyser's band doing "Who Wouldn't Love You," which we played a hundred times and hummed along. Mom said it would be fun to dance but nobody got up.

Moving day, today, almost everything went right. The truck came on time, the furniture got loaded into it with bumping and noise that made Mom nervous but nothing was broken, Mr. Meyerson brought over the Daily News himself for Dad so he could shake his hand goodbye, Mrs. Macilenny made sandwiches for everybody for lunch, and then the one thing happened that didn't go right. The factory owner's car and driver came late because of a flat tire and when I climbed into the rear seat and looked through the window, there was Rhoda standing at the curb, clutching her school books, looking right at me, biting her lip.

I said, "Oh," which she couldn't hear and the car started off. I told myself I would not look back but I couldn't help it and the owner's car was a Cadillac with a big, square rear window so you can see a long way and I knew Rhoda was seeing my face pasted to the window while I watched her face, lip-biting still, shrink in the distance, like in some movies when people part, with violins playing, only this happened in an awful silence.

We turned a corner finally and Mom said, "This is not an ending. You two will be lifelong friends."

I shook my head. How could she know that? "Trust me," she said, reading my expression. "You'll find the ways."

A mixed-up bunch of pictures skipped through my head, phone calls, trips with Mom to meet and shop together at Macy's, high school when we could travel on our own, lunches between two married women, comparing kids, then grand-kids, then two old women rocking in a nursing home, shouting because they're hard of hearing—it got silly and I must have smiled because Mom did, too, and I felt a little better.

I'm feeling even better now in my new room, because of Dad. He brought in a corrugated box of my stuff, glanced around the room and out the window, murmured, "Hmm," at the sight of the girls across the street, and said as he walked out, "These houses are all two years old."

Why tell me that again? We've talked about it—oh.

In his own way, he shows me more respect than anyone else does. He can refer to me as little girl, and pat my cheek, and supervise my comic book reading, yet he's willing to give me a clue about something important, just a clue, trusting me to figure out the rest of it so it will mean more than if he simply tells me.

I figure it out.

If these houses are all two years old, every girl across the street came here from someplace else, and not very long ago. Suppose

I ask where that someplace was, casually, just part of the conversation. Each of us relives her experience and bingo!—I'm not from some other planet; in fact, we're all in the same club, just like that.

I collect my comic books, run a wet comb through that bale of straw on my head and go downstairs.

Gonna lay my burden down, down by the riverside,
Gonna put on my starry crown, down by the riverside…

The Marble King

It was no surprise to me that Herb left high school a millionaire. Even in fourth grade, he knew how to turn a profit. There's no malice in my saying that. I actually liked him and as for the rest of the gang, they readily accepted him. He was a naturally cheerful boy and by the leadership standards of prepubescent males, all physical prowess and noise, a pudgy, uncoordinated kid was certainly no threat to anyone. Indeed, how could you turn away someone who made you feel superior?

For some of us there was a sympathy factor, too. Herb's father ran off when Herb was four, his mother died suddenly a year later and he was taken in by cousins who provided shelter and little more. I tried to imagine a home without a mother or a father and couldn't.

We were all town dwellers then, so one of the favorite pastimes was marbles, the old fashioned pavement game where you'd aim a marble to hit the other guy's. Not as easy as it appeared, it

The Marble King and Other Stories

required a little snap of the thumb that would make a marble roll, not bounce, a smooth backswing of the wrist, what baseball players call follow through, and a clever little spin on your marble (with some body English to make sure it was noticed).

Lacking such skills, Herb was a steady loser and his stock of marbles shrank each day. He shook his head stoically.

Boyhood games run in cycles, of course, and the day came when shooting a marble at other marbles began to pall. That was the day Herb showed up carrying an empty shoebox. He set it down carefully against the garage wall that served as a backstop. A hole had been cut at the bottom of one side of the box, big enough it seemed for even a Boulder—the largest size marble—to slide in comfortably.

Herb let us look at the inviting target for a minute, then hesitatingly announced that he would give two marbles for each marble we could roll into the box. Naturally, he would keep any marble that missed. He gave us his usual nervous smile. I'm not sure I can do this, the smile said, but if it's what the gang wants, I'm okay with it.

The cycle was short, only two days. Being mocked by a hole in a shoebox grows tiresome quickly. For Herb, two days were enough. His pockets and two string bags bulged with marbles when the sun set on the second day. He managed to look apologetic, except once when our eyes met. He had seen me regarding the hole, bigger than a Boulder, yes, but only a direct hit could enter. A glancing blow that would win a marble in the regular game simply caromed off the cardboard here, into Herb's pocket.

He winked. Nothing triumphant in it, nothing spiteful in it, just a touch of merriment. As I said, I liked him and so would anyone, I believe, at that moment. I blew him a little Bronx cheer, pffffft! in return and that exchange became a private greeting for us, lasting into high school whenever we passed each other.

172

THE MARBLE KING

He was into his study guide business by then. Unlike the shoe-box game, there was nothing deceptive, at least not yet. He enlisted four of the brighter—and lonelier—girls, wisely made them partners in the enterprise (15 percent each, the remaining 40 percent his) and steered them into preparing simple two-page "Hints From Herb" about upcoming English and History assignments or tests.

They were legitimate in that they did not provide answers directly. However, they did point students to the passages of a textbook or novel where the answers could be found, even highlighting key words or phrases and—for the thicker-skulled—adding a margin note here and there such as, *Does this indicate the novel is* **satire**? Or *Was Charlemagne* **merciful** *to the people he conquered?* And for the essay writers, *Is this a useful passage to illustrate the book's theme?*

This was nothing the better teachers didn't provide in class but one of Herb's writers was also a budding cartoonist, a girl named Cassie, a member of the student council. I was council president and welcomed her presence. She was a listener and we already had enough talkers, mostly compulsive. Cassie sprinkled cheerleaders and football helmets and rock guitars in the guide pages, stamping Herb's "Hints" immediately as a student-to-student, peer-to-peer enterprise

As such, it carried an unwritten "hint" for the naturally rebellious teen spirit: Teachers? Really? We can do it better!

Herb leveraged that feeling. Whispers began, claiming the guides were more useful than classroom instruction. A campaign followed—remarks uttered openly within earshot of teachers, anonymous notes in faculty mailboxes, guides taped on classroom doors reading, Cut Class, This Is All You Need—a campaign stirred along by Herb and his staff, joined gleefully by the crowd of agitators common to every school.

The exception was Cassie. I noticed her telling students to stop being infantile; the guides were a nice extra but that's all. I was impressed by her outspokenness; I had always considered her shy.

"Why don't you just quit the study guide staff?" I asked after a student council meeting.

"I thought about it, but he's Herb, you know—" She twisted a stray ringlet of brown hair seeking an answer. Finally, she said, "Could *you* abandon him?"

I admitted that I couldn't.

I adamantly refused to help him, though, when he tried to enlist me in the rising chorus. Herb was a junior then and I was a senior, a privileged rank, with the added influence of the student council post.

"Well, I'm only asking that you bring it up at the next meeting," he argued. "Offer any opinion you want. Just the mention will keep the pot simmering." His wink followed. I skipped the Bronx cheer, my suspicions suddenly confirmed about why he wanted to incite school officials. They had been no problem so far, accepting the guides, some teachers even praising them.

"But if you won't," he went on, "I understand. You could have speeded things up for me but you can't derail it. Human nature, Jeff, human nature. But I'm glad for your attitude. I admire it, actually. You're going on for a divinity degree, aren't you? You'll be preaching salvation to me." He chuckled.

"That's the purpose." I didn't chuckle. "Where will you go?"

"Business school, of course. Harvard or Yale. I have a lot to teach them."

The wink followed. I gave him the Bronx cheer this time.

And, as with the shoebox, human nature bowed again to Herb's manipulation. School officials had their fill of the daily taunts and banned the guides. Herb immediately showed up at

THE MARBLE KING

every TV station and newspaper, innocently wondering if the First Amendment had been violated. Are young people of this community being denied free speech? Are constitutional rights being ignored by the very people we depend on to teach them? As journalists, what do you think?

When the dust settled, "Hints From Herb" were not only restored in our own Davenport high school, they went national. From a quarter each in Davenport, which probably grossed Herb and his writers about three thousand a term, they rose to fifty cents each and the gross multiplied by a hundred times at a guess.

Sufficient in any event for Senior Scholastic Magazine to buy the rights from Herb for an unreported seven-figure sum. He had kept the copyright in his name alone but his partners were not heard to complain. They had enough by graduation for flashy new wardrobes and equally flashy new cars, quickly followed by devoted attentions from boys who previously ignored them.

Again, Cassie was the exception. Although she had blossomed into a rosy prettiness in her senior year, she didn't flaunt it in any way, no flashy car appeared in her driveway and she seemed to prefer being alone, a fact my mother mentioned pointedly during one of our weekly phone calls. I was in my freshman year at Trinity in northern Illinois, and she made it her mission to keep me up to date on home town happenings.

"I wonder why," I said. "Cassie's an attractive girl, I know she's intelligent from our student council days and her cartoons tell you about her great sense of humor."

I heard only the hum of the telephone line. Sometimes a mother's silence will reveal a lot.

The wedding took place three years later. I was entering seminary, where family housing is provided. Reviewing Cassie's invitation list, I found Herb's name.

"Herb? All the way from California?"

He was established now as a prominent venture capitalist in Silicon Valley. Harvard and Yale had gotten by without him. Coming out of high school with a fortune in hand and this exciting, youth-hungry boom town just begging for smart investors, why waste four years in a classroom?

Our only contact during these years had been scattered emails. My messages were headed with Scripture verses about salvation or God's grace which he ignored, except once when he wrote, "Jeff, I'm doing wonderfully well in this valley and it was created by nutty, long-haired nerds, not by God. But keep on preaching, keep on being who you are." I did, of course, and he kept ignoring it and so the cyber talk we actually exchanged revolved around the high school football team's winning season or the sun in California or the food in the college cafeteria, the casual stuff I shared with a dozen other former school mates. Not so casual to Herb, though, judging by Cassie's answer.

"He'd come all the way from Tasmania if he had to. In fact, he'd be terribly upset if we didn't invite him. It would be pulling away one of the pillars of his life."

"Isn't that a bit dramatic?"

"When we were doing the study guides, he'd say, 'Let me read this the way Jeffrey would read it.' Your approval meant more than anyone else's."

"That was then, Cassie. He's a millionaire many times over today."

She was thoughtful for a moment, then said, "When you were a kid, you could catch a fly ball like all your friends, couldn't you?"

THE MARBLE KING

I got the point. I was thinking like someone who fit in easily. But if you're someone who doesn't fit in, you exist in a treacherous world, pitfalls everywhere. Years wouldn't erase the importance of someone you consider reliable, especially the only one with whom you shared a private communication. A wink and a Bronx cheer. I imagine friendships have been founded on less.

Herb sat in the last pew during the ceremony, drawing a steady little wave of turning heads. Cassie raised an eyebrow at me in amusement at one point. Shouldn't the bride be the center of attention?

But these sidelong glances were as far as most of the guests cared to go. When we moved to one of the restaurants on the riverfront for the reception, instead of crowding around this hometown-boy-turned-tycoon as I expected, people stayed distant, intimidated perhaps by such wealth, or in the case of ex-classmates, suitably embarrassed at a sudden show of camaraderie for this boy they had ignored or teased for years. Only his former study guide partners, all married now, involved him in any conversation, their husbands standing by uneasily. Former teachers avoided him openly, memories of the study guide still rankling. For the most part, Herb sat or wandered the room quietly, sampling the food and drink, a fixed smile on his face. Near the end of the afternoon I saw him through the window, standing alone on the waterside patio, gazing at the ever-tidal, ever-busy Mississippi.

I joined him there when most of the guests were leaving and Cassie was freshening up for our own departure. Herb appeared comfortable for the first time that day. He stood close—inside, he seemed to be leaning away from the few people he spoke to—and drew in a long, unhurried breath. He blew it out with a little whistle.

177

"Why should anybody love this contrary old river," he remarked like a man talking about the family dog.

"Because it's home," I answered, "and for me, the only large body of water I know."

"You could see San Francisco Bay if you want. Pacific Ocean, too. There's a big job coming up. Yours if you like."

I laughed. "Me, in Silicon Valley. What's the punch line?"

He kept his eyes on a tug powering a trio of barges upriver.

"I don't have a punch line. I have a serious offer. You're at this turning point in your life and you should think of every option. Next month, just when you're supposed to start seminary, two electronic game companies are going to merge. I know because I'm the major stockholder in each. The resulting company will need a CEO. You, if you choose. Name your salary."

I stared at him. He watched a lone gull settle on a barge.

"You want a twenty-two year old with a Bible degree and no business experience to be a CEO," I said. "I'm still looking for a punch line."

"I'm only twenty-one," he responded. "Forget age. Silicon Valley is driven by guys in their early twenties." He looked at me now. "And most of them haven't had the business courses you have. Shall I list them all? I haven't really pried, you know."

I shrugged. Trinity's curriculum is public information as is their goal of a well rounded graduate, not just a theologian.

"And more. Those high school student council meetings." He covered his ears and rolled his eyes. If I could manage a crowd of squirrely teenagers, I could manage people anywhere.

It was my turn to watch the barges as I tried to shape an answer.

"We could add some stock to the salary," he said.

"You mean stock suddenly worth a lot more because of the merger," I answered. "And the number one beneficiary of that will be…?"

He snapped a thumb and finger, shooting an imaginary marble. "Naturally. And if you're thinking I invested in these companies with this in mind, you're right. Don't sniff at it, Jeff. Like the shoebox and the study guides, it's all out in the open. No Ponzi scheme, no con games, just a business merger, in public."

"All engineered quietly by the major shareholder. There's always that little twist." My tone was not as sharp as the words. This was a happy occasion and I was certainly not going to mar it for any of us. And truthfully, it was difficult to rebuke Herb; he hadn't changed since the shoebox. No spite, no arrogance, no boastfulness at his accomplishments, and if the merriment of the boy with the marbles had ripened into the satisfaction of the man with the stock portfolio, it was still candid and matter-of-fact.

"That little twist," he echoed. "That means you're going to lecture me about Rock'em Rabbit, aren't you?" He held his hands up as if to ward off a blow.

The most successful of the products he backed, Rock'em Rabbit challenged players to work their way through a labyrinth based on skill and memory, except for a random factor. The right combination of backward moves, found by pure chance, would cue the appearance of a giant rabbit that crashed through the barriers and carried a player to victory.

Nothing but gambling, a casino for kids, claimed critics. Herb assumed, correctly, that I agreed.

"But think of this," he went on. "The game *can* be won by skill alone. Nobody has to try the rabbit moves. And those moves take you in reverse, costing time and space. Like an investment, is it worth it? Kids are learning about choices."

It was time for the Bronx cheer and I gave him one loud enough to turn a few heads among departing guests. "Something they teach in seminary," Herb called to them and I couldn't help joining the laughter. When it died away, Herb was looking at me seriously again.

"You'll turn the job down, I suppose. You won't be CEO of a company that makes Rock'em Rabbit."

"That's not the main reason."

"No, it wouldn't be. You're determined to be in ministry?"

"I'm called to be in ministry."

"You're the only one I ever met who could say that and not sound pretentious. But it won't be like that"—he waved in the direction of our big downtown wedding church—"a modern chapel kept up by big-city money, new pews, new sound system, everything. I know those countryside churches where young preachers start out. That's where you'll go, isn't it?"

I nodded.

"Beat-up old clapboard," he continued, "rattling pipes, drafty Sunday School rooms, maybe a little Christian academy with twenty kids at hand-me down desks from the public school."

"And probably a fractious congregation," I added, "arguing over hymn selection, deacon appointments, the Christmas play, who knows what else?"

"And that's what you want?"

"That's where I'll be needed."

"Where will you be needed?" Cassie's voice was at my shoulder.

"At the little church in the cornfield," Herb said. "Don't you have a honeymoon to go on? Stop blabbing with me and take off."

I glanced around as we drove away. He had his hands behind his head, leaning back contentedly, taking a deep breath of the contrary old river.

THE MARBLE KING

"He would have kept his word if I said yes," I told Cassie. "I'd be a CEO."

"And Herb would have been crushed. But he really didn't expect a yes from you."

"It was a test, then?"

"To make sure Jeff was still Jeff and the world was in place."

"Jeff the pure. Jeff the incorruptible. He has this idealized image of me—"

"It's real. I just married it."

"—shush—this idealized image, and it's so important to him, yet he lives in this cynical world of stock deals and Rock'em Rabbit games."

"With his talents, what else could he do?"

"Nothing that wouldn't frustrate him, I suppose. Still the kid with the shoebox."

We were south of the city, driving by a string of exclusive homes and I said, "Cassie?"

"Hmm?"

"You realize I deprived you of a luxurious life style. No home like those"—I gestured—"no San Francisco shopping and theater, just the little church in the cornfield."

"I'll need some recipes," she said. "Let's see." She began counting on her fingers. "Corn chowder, corn bread, corn muffins, corn pudding, corn casserole, corn fritters, cornmeal mush, corn tortillas, corn and bean salad, did I leave anything out?"

I have never, for even a solitary second, regretted marrying Cassie.

The Marble King and Other Stories

No cornfield as it turned out, but a church on the edge of a town of two thousand, with a view of a feed house and a dairy farm from the church rear windows, plus an intruder into the pastoral landscape: a collection of new homes and garden apartments in construction beyond the farm. More, news around town had it that the dairy farmer was ready to sell and development would soon cross his field right to the church door.

An ethanol processor and a medical instrument manufacturer had arrived nearby in the last two years, rejuvenating the dormant little village. My congregants' heads danced with visions of growing membership, a renovated building, maybe even a new one, and a modernized Christian academy. Herb had been right about the little school with the twenty students and the hand-me-down desks.

The visions were reasonable. This was a vigorous church. One look around Sunday morning and you knew it. Instead of the Sunday shuffle seen in far too many churches, people here seemed to trot in, calling to one another, shaking hands, exchanging hugs, swirling around like a cicada storm, settling into pews in one cheerful, collective body that radiated energy.

It was not the church Cassie and I gingerly entered ten years ago. The outgoing pastor, a soft-spoken man in his fifties, happily on his way to a faculty post at a Bible college, compared the church he was bequeathing us to a complacent family: it's loving, yes—a member's illness brings a deluge of help with meals and errands and child care—but it's quarrelsome—jaws clench over who gets what committee appointment or which color to paint the nursery—and it's jealous—there's a lot of sniffing and muttering when other churches get more space in the Pulpit Happenings page of the local paper—and, needless to say, it's resistant to change.

182

"Suppose," he said, "just suppose, there's a teenager with a guitar, a talented boy, and he wants to accompany on Sunday mornings along with the piano. Plays acoustic guitar, nice sweet sound, no rock stuff. The deacons, all of them older members, say no, piano's fine. Telling them guitars are common in church now doesn't move them. Should the pastor give it up?"

"No, he has to keep on. With prayer. With patience. With perseverance."

"Exactly," he agreed. "I wish you well. The boy's name is Freddie."

Freddie is music director today. There are three guitars and a drum set as well as the piano. Contemporary Christian music mixes with hymns each week and everyone sings out joyously. Jaws remain unclenched over committee appointments and the color of the nursery—or when to hold the church picnic or how much of the budget goes to missionaries or the choice of the cast of the Christmas play. A publicity director makes sure there's a steady flow of announcements in Pulpit Happenings, helped by Cassie's cartoons.

There's the occasional stifled murmur or the glance at the ceiling at a decision; I'm not a miracle worker. "Only a student council president," Cassie says, but with God's grace, it's working. We even have two younger men among the deacons and six new families in the congregation. I look out at the eager and responsive faces and listen to the excited buzz and chatter on Sunday mornings and know I face a congregation ready to expand.

Without the means to do it. When a pastor can count six new families over the course of his ten years, he's obviously leading a small flock. We had eighty members, typical of a town our size, and an annual budget of one hundred thousand dollars, enough to hold steady, a success by today's standards, yet frustrating for a congregation that sees a potential harvest reaching right to the doorstep. Yes, God will provide a way if that's His will, but aren't we His instruments?

One of the younger deacons went on his own to the dairy farmer and asked if he would sell us a few adjacent acres apart from his other deal. That would give us space for a new building and parking. "He said he'd be happy to," the deacon told me glumly, "at fifteen thousand an acre."

The other young deacon inquired at local banks about the possibility of a loan. The refusals were polite, even sympathetic, the most he could report.

Members who worked in construction and carpentry prowled the auditorium seeking a way to add space, looking baffled when they couldn't find one. Others tried to work out a plan for two Sunday services but had no answer for Sunday school, the youth program, the Christian academy, prayer meetings, luncheons, weddings, baptisms, the many things that bring cohesiveness and unity to a rural church.

All this deserved my full attention. Enough frustration will turn even the strongest congregation to bitterness and scapegoating; the very character of this church I loved was threatened.

But I had another worry and it was growing. There had been no contact from Herb for a month, climaxing a year in which his email had become hasty and indifferent.

The wedding day conversation had kicked our friendship into a higher gear. Our messages became chatty and filled with detail: his business ventures, the oddball characters of Silicon Valley, the house with a view of San Francisco Bay (t'ain't the Mississippi but all they got here), his dating (hadn't met a girl he really trusted)—and from my end, griping about the pressure of seminary classes, then the anecdotes about being a new pastor (the navy blue tie left on the lectern, a comment on my stripes and plaids), and in time, news and pictures of the children; we had two boys and a girl now and Herb insisted like a favorite uncle on steady reports. He had sent a thousand dollar bond for each when they were born. Start a college fund and don't argue with me, he wrote.

I kept the word of God in my email, sending him favorite verses, sometimes entire sermons if they dealt with salvation. He either ignored them or made such comments as "A rip-snorter of a message, brother" or "They gotta love this stuff in Iowa!"

Our spiritual gap aside, the conversation was frequent and warm, with genuine interest from each of us in the life of the other, until messages started to arrive that were brief and detached—'a lot of work to do, will catch up when I get a break' or 'thanks for the pic of Tommy, more later'—that sort of thing and the 'more later' never came.

On a hunch, I started checking the stock market and Silicon Valley news. The holding company Herb had established for his enterprises was in the middle of a merger, with Herb agreeing to sell his shares and not at the best price. "Seems like a hurried sale," said one business writer.

"Why don't you call him again," Cassie urged when I told her. I had tried that a week ago and reached a secretary who said she would let him know.

I reached her again, got the same answer and said, "Tell him I need to speak to the marble king."

"What?"

"He'll understand, just tell him that."

Herb phoned that night. Cassie and I were in the kitchen together and she put her head close to join in.

Herb greeted us with, "Good evening, cornfield dwellers. The king has heard your petition and will grant you an audience." His voice was weak and slightly hoarse in counterpoint to the bantering words.

The Marble King and Other Stories

"Hello, your majesty. You've ignored your Iowa subjects for a while. How are you?"

"Well, in truth there's less majesty to admire these days."

"You found a good weight loss program?"

"More like it found me." He paused, then, "Jeff, I'm coming back to Davenport." The bantering tone was gone abruptly.

"Good," I said, feeling a little chill of bad news ahead. "I'm only an hour away. We'll be able to spend some time together."

"Yeah. For a few months, anyway."

Cassie gripped my arm. We were having the same thought.

"Your mother?" she said, hesitant, recalling the sudden death when Herb was a boy.

"Yeah. Same thing. Body's riddled with it. I always knew I was vulnerable but maybe twenty, thirty years away. I'm younger than she was when it happened. Go figure."

"When will you be here?" I asked.

"The first of the month. I'm renting an apartment on the waterfront. No point in my asking you not to bring a Bible, I suppose."

Cassie replied, keeping a cheerful tone despite misty eyes. "Four years in Bible college, three years in seminary, ten years an ordained minister. He's a Bible with legs. And it will be good for you."

Herb laughed, a weary sound. "Alright, alright, the price I have to pay for his company."

We sat on the apartment terrace, enjoying the river's after-dark show—the bobbing lamps of pleasure boats close in, the crisscrossing beacons of larger craft midriver, the reflected lights of the Centennial Bridge turning the water to polished amber.

Herb's cousins—the couple who took him in as a boy, both elderly and slow-moving now—had left after bringing a huge basket of flowers and looking on helplessly. A night duty nurse arrived, a starched and grandmotherly woman who counted out pills for him and frowned at Herb's sitting in the 'damp river air,' although it was a balmy mid-May evening. He let her drape a shawl over his shoulders, calling her a tyrant. She patted his shoulder and went inside to the TV.

I waved downriver and asked Herb if he remembered Mr. Bentley and his dawn patrol. Bentley was an English teacher who advised us regularly to walk here when sunrise sent its rays leaping upstream like salmon, or trout, or shooting stars, depending on his poetic whim. As I intended, it started a chain of school day reminiscences that took us well into the night. I had decided no preaching, not on this first meeting. Better to ease into it.

The nurse came out, tapping her wristwatch when I was in the middle of the frog dissection tale. Ninth and tenth grade biology lab, all the guys standing around, paralyzed by the idea, and this petite, baby faced blond girl –

"Betsy," Herb said, starting to laugh.

"Betsy, yes, she grabbed a scalpel and dug into her specimen like a Christmas roast while the fullback on the football team put a hand over his mouth and ran for the door."

Herb's laughter rose and precipitately ended in a rattling cough that bent him over and brought the nurse hurrying out with a bottle of suppressant. This evidently happened regularly. We helped him inside and as I felt his thin, shaking shoulders under the shawl, I knew I would be talking about salvation tomorrow. Time was short

We sat companionably on the terrace again, eyes often closed against the morning sun, absorbing the river's drowsy anthem of boat horns and calling shore birds. During a lull, I began to recite softly from the Gospel of John.

"Hallelujah," Herb muttered, and so began a daily routine of my reading and talking about salvation while he regarded the water or the sky or his hands or shut his eyes in a show of absent-mindedly tolerating me. He heard, though. There were the occasional jibing remarks as in the emails—"Shouldn't there be some organ music at this point?"—and a flow of skeptical grunts.

I simply moved ahead quietly with the readings I had prepared the night before: Scripture passages or the writings of the great evangelists, no more than half an hour or so at a time—I sensed the limits—and avoiding eternal-lake-of-fire warnings for this dying man—but by the second week, some testiness crept into his responses anyway.

"You really think you're going to save my soul?" he asked acidly. "Come on, Jeff."

"God will do that, not me. I'm the messenger."

"Preachers," he sighed. "Always an answer."

The rest of the week he shifted every few minutes in his chair or puffed out sharp breaths at my readings or shook his head impatiently when I told stories of congregation members and classmates who had come to embrace Jesus and salvation.

He boiled over at the outset of the next week. I was reading from the grand Jonathan Edwards sermon, *A Divine and Supernatural Light*, and Edwards' words about "the blindness" and "the "dark and deluded apprehensions" of the unsaved brought Herb struggling to sit upright.

"Stop it," he called out and his hoarse voice shook. "I'm not blind, I'm not deluded. I see very clearly a god who took a father from me at four, a god who took a mother from me at five, a god who made me fat and awkward, a god who made me the kid who didn't belong and gave me years of loneliness you think you can imagine but you can't, nobody can, and a god, finally, who gave me this." He ran a hand over his sunken cheeks and blanketed, wasting body. "If you see anything else, you're the deluded one."

"Herb," I said as quietly as I could. I leaned close and took one of his thin hands in both of mine.

"What?" he said, trying to pull away but I held him.

"This is the God who gave you a shoebox."

He looked quizzically at me.

"This is the God who gave you a pocketknife."

The look turned wary; he was quick enough to see where I was leading.

"And Herb, this is the God who gave you the wits to take the pocketknife and carve a hole in the shoe box just the right size."

I released him and he sank back. He turned his head to look upriver and I couldn't see his face. After a long silence, he said, "I always wanted a boat like that when I was a kid." He pointed to a catamaran crossing the current toward the island. His voice was tight; he was forcing himself to be calm. "Joey Moore's family had one. I used to watch them launch it."

"The Moores bragged it would never capsize," I replied lightly, "and it nearly drowned them all." I was content to let him take us back into reminiscing. He'd shown anger, the signal that he had been reached, a signal I welcomed. Indifference is the enemy that can't be moved; it's like poking a sleeping hippo. But anger, an emotional display—that could be grappled with and moved.

"He'll be angry again next time," Cassie said that night. "He can't deny what you said about the shoebox, God's gift of cleverness, and that's liable to be scary, threatening a life-long conviction."

"And that brings on anger, yes. I have the soft answers, you know." I tapped the Bible on my desk.

"You're thinking of anger as shouting, the typical reaction. This is Herb you're dealing with. Better keep your wits about you."

Cassie was prescient.

After fifteen minutes of my reading the next day, Herb, who had been listening quietly, even looking agreeable, interrupted me.

"I offered you a job once," he said.

"I remember it well," I answered cautiously.

He rested his chin on his hands and regarded me. His eyes, usually clouded these days, were bright.

"I have another offer. This time it's not for you. I know better. It's for your congregation. Two million dollars. I keep up with the local news. A whole new town is springing up around you. Two million buys a new church building, a school, a gym for the community to use, a counseling center, you name it."

"It's a conditional offer, isn't it?" I closed the Bible with exaggerated care. "I stop preaching to you, right?"

I was pleased yesterday; I was jubilant today. If Herb was willing to spend two million dollars to keep the message at bay, he was truly battling with it now, battling hard.

"Exactly." He gave me that deliberately apologetic smile from the fourth grade days—I hope I'm doing the right thing—while his index fingers aimed at me like naval guns, challenging.

"You know I won't agree."

"The offer is to your church. You're obligated to tell your deacons. It's sure to leak out to the whole congregation. Then what?"

"I talk to them. I tell them it has to be turned down. This"—I lifted the Bible—"explains *why* it has to be turned down. Then I come back here and we resume."

THE MARBLE KING

Any pastor who thinks he *knows* his congregation, really knows their hearts, is misguided. I made that discovery, to my astonishment, at the deacons' meeting. The two young deacons actually clapped their hands as I finished. One of the older deacons, a man who could quote Scripture better than I, pursed his lips—I could sense his wavering—and then inclined his head in agreement at the younger men.

The remaining older deacons, three of them, saw more deeply. "We're looking at the devil's trap," said one. "Pastor Jeff has to press on."

"And leave how many souls unsaved out there?" asked the youngest man. He gestured with both hands at the fields.

"Think of it," put in his comrade. "We could be getting a hundred new members, two hundred maybe. We'll be the most inviting, most active church between here and the city. I know he's a boyhood friend of yours, Pastor, but—"

What had I been teaching these past ten years, I asked myself. I made a mental bow, too, towards Herb's instincts about human nature. Better than mine, obviously. But I did have a bit of unarguable logic on my side.

"The boyhood friendship is not the motive," I said. "The boyhood friendship is the bridge. I believe I'm the only one who can cross it and the Lord is using me that way."

"And so He's sacrificing all the others we might reach?" came the reply.

So much for unarguable logic. Let's try God's Word.

"Matthew 18:12," I said to the Scripture expert, "and Luke 15:8 to 10."

Reluctantly but dutifully he recited the parable of the lost sheep and its injunction to leave the flock and save the wanderer—and the similar parable of the lost silver coin. I repeated the closing of the silver coin verses:

191

"I tell you, there is rejoicing in the presence of the angels of God over one sinner who repents." I held a finger up. "One," I said. "One sinner."

The youngest deacon objected, "Well, the parables only talk about the stray sheep or the missing coin and they don't say anything about potential, like sheep that are not in your flock today or coins you might earn later—" He trailed off doubtfully, seeking a linkage that wasn't quite there. But I recognized that heels were being dug in here.

"I've done what I'm obliged to do by informing you," I announced. "With your agreement, I'll close the meeting with a prayer for wisdom. We can then go home for individual meditation."

With uncertain glances at me, they bowed their heads.

The following day, Sunday, I faced a lot of nervous motion in the pews, some of the members smiling at me deliberately, others staring fixedly, still others looking off, avoiding my eyes.

I had shelved my original sermon overnight and instead told the story of Balaam, the rent-a-prophet in the Book of Numbers. "A man who would say what he was paid to say," I declared, "do as he was paid to do and willingly, knowingly, oppose God's will."

There were those who nodded in approval, half the gathering or more, and yet too many who remained expressionless. Standing at the front door for goodbyes, the division repeated itself— half the departers, probably more, shaking my hand with meaningful firmness, praising the sermon, while others slipped by wordlessly, and a sizeable number chose to exit at the side door.

We took the children to the zoo on the Illinois side in the afternoon, an hour and a half away, and then to a restaurant, intentionally filling the time until nightfall. Herb's cousins usually came Sunday, so we'd have no time for quiet talk there, and I didn't want to be at home for visits or phone calls from the congregation. Sheltering the rest of the family from the turbulence was on my mind, as well as avoiding private conversations. Not that I was unwilling to talk, just that conversations are so often mis-remembered and mis-reported.

I expected a restless night, a sign that even ministers can falter in their faith. But at bedtime, after sitting outside and praying beneath a starry Iowa sky, the tension lifted, and so quickly I needed some deep, comfortable breaths to convince myself it was gone. In its place, a tranquility came that eased me back inside and into an immediate, undisturbed sleep.

In the morning, the tranquility remained, edged with growing anticipation. I had to force myself to keep at the speed limit driving to the city.

Herb spied the mood the instant I walked out on the terrace. Bundled to the neck in a blanket, with a wool cap tucked over his ears, only his face showed, even a bit thinner than yesterday it seemed, although his eyes were quick and watchful.

"You have a triumphant clergyman before you," he told the nurse as she curled the blanket around his ankles. "And stop fussing so. It's July, you know."

She ignored him and said to me, "I'll be in the kitchen if he needs anything." She murmured as she passed me, "Troubled night. He hardly slept." I made a sympathetic sound and turned to hide the slight smile.

I sat facing Herb and we exchanged long, appraising looks.

"You knew I'd be back," I said finally.

"As of this morning, I did. I had some doubt before that. Would you really reject a gift for other people?"

"You realized it was not a gift."

He shrugged. "A snare. I suppose I knew it all along. Another Rock'em Rabbit."

The Marble King and Other Stories

"Am I hearing a drop of repentance?"

He made no response. A dragonfly, glinting gold in the sun, floated by and our eyes followed it out of sight.

"You're so full of confidence," Herb said. "Didn't you have a difficult weekend?"

"Manageable."

"Your congregation knows?"

"I made it clear I would be here."

"And they approved?"

"A lot of them, maybe sixty percent at a guess, mostly the older ones. The rest are frustrated and resentful."

He waved a hand dismissively. "You've got the majority. You're okay."

"Churches don't work that way. A divided congregation becomes like a dysfunctional family, forever battling, laying blame, often splitting into two hostile churches."

"But you—you can bring them together. I know you."

"It's not the student council. A pastor has a chance when the problem is from outside but when a decision by the pastor himself is the cause, the resentment is an open wound and he has only one option: leave and let someone new do the healing."

Herb looked alarmed. "I remember your emails, you love that congregation—"

"I always will—"

"—and after ten years, it's uprooting your life, Cassie's—"

"We're prepared."

"She'd be giving up a home she must treasure by now. And the kids? Eleven, nine, seven, old enough to have friendships, a familiar school—"

"Old enough to know they're loved and with God's mercy, three sociable, outgoing kids who will make new friends quickly."

"You're trying to make it sound easy and it can't be. It's a sacrifice, a big one. Why would I let you make it? It's certainly not what I intended when I made that money offer."

"You can't stop it."

His face tightened stubbornly. "I can't? I simply say go home, Jeff, don't come back."

"You can't," I said, and I heard my voice steady and assured. "You can't because inside the two men sitting on this terrace are the two boys who once played marbles on the sidewalk."

When you examined that, it made no sense at all.

Except that right here it made perfect sense.

The stubbornness faded. "Fourth grade," he said, eyes closing, looking inward, seeing it, hand curling to cup something and to heft it. A bag of marbles. The shape was unmistakeable.

He opened his eyes and said, "Alright. No more games. Let's begin."

Cassie and I watched a touch football free-for-all through the kitchen window of our new parsonage. She tapped a loose pane.

"On my list," I assured her. "Number twenty-three, I think."

"Are they playing by any rules out there?" she asked.

A swirling anarchy of children's bodies filled the yard, including our own three, some of their new friends whom we recognized and about two dozen more who were still just faces in the pews.

"You throw the ball and yell," I answered. "All the rules you need. And it keeps them warm"

"Warm, good idea." Cassie took my hand and pressed it against the loose pane to feel the chilly October wind knifing through.

"Right, tomorrow, as soon as I get back."

'Get back' would be from Davenport, a trip I had to take in response to a letter from the attorney handling Herb's estate. The will had gone through probate and my presence was requested at the reading. I faced that with surprise and some embarrassment. I certainly wanted no gifts.

The van jounced on the uneven driveway as I left in the morning. I mentally added pothole filling to the list. There'd be help from the congregation; it was a common driveway for the weathered old church building and the cottage, equally weathered, that served as a parsonage.

I liked it. Cassie did, too. The repairs were all things I could handle with patience and both house and church exuded that ageless, farm-country assurance: we've given you one century and we're ready to give you another, no worry.

Beyond the yard that provided a touch football arena lay a stream where crayfish and minnows lured children, and then some twenty acres of corn, only withered stalks now but promising a rich, green abundance come July, shoulder high, filling the view from our cottage.

Alright Herb, we found that little church in a cornfield.

And the church lived up to *my* forecast that day—disputes over hymn selection, deacon appointments, the church picnic locale, all the familiar stuff that made me want to say, You people have no idea of what a real congregational fracture is like. I held it in, grateful to be confronting troubles I could resolve, and quickly, the advantage of the second time around.

The attorney gathered us at a conference table in a paneled room—the cousins, a scattering of other family members, myself, and the chairman of the board of deacons at my former church. I regarded him with obvious surprise. He shrugged, palms up. It was a mystery to him why he was here. A glance flashed between us, though. Reading of a will meant only one thing.

The bequests began with the family. Herb had been generous. The cousins and even the more distant relatives would now be wealthy people. The cousins appeared grateful and the others ranged from stunned to satisfied.

The attorney went on to other names and I heard them as one hears an echo, first the sound, then the recognition.

My children's names.

A sum of five hundred thousand dollars in trust for their higher education.

I became one with the relatives who sat stunned.

The attorney announced the name of my former church.

A gift of two million dollars.

The deacon joined the stunned contingent. He suspected some gift, but this?

The attorney was going on, "There *is* one provision to this bequest." The deacon and I both stiffened. "A provision that the church place an engraved plaque of a modest size, three feet by three feet, in a prominent position in the vestibule of any new auditorium, said plaque to honor Pastor Jeffrey Cardin for his vision and leadership and for providing the inspiration for this building."

"However," the reading carried on, "Pastor Cardin may veto this provision if he chooses."

"I choose," I told the attorney. "I definitely veto the plaque." I repeated it to make certain.

"I veto the plaque."

"No plaque," he agreed, making a notation, handing me a pen to initial it. Holding the pen steady was not easy, I was shaking so much with suppressed laughter.

The deacon and I stopped to talk in the parking lot afterwards. He was one of the older men who had supported me.

"Guess your friend didn't know Baptist churches don't go in for plaques," he said. "Thanks. Did you have any idea he intended to give us this money?"

The Marble King and Other Stories

"No, and I should have seen it. I had three weeks with him after he was saved."

"Ah. Painful and joyful at once, I'm guessing."

I spent a moment reliving those days, the emaciated body, the deepening comprehension, Cassie joining us, reading to him –

"I'll remember it," I answered. "For a lifetime."

"Yes," he said, waiting for me to blink the memory away, then, "Any message I can take back to the congregation? A lot of us miss you."

"And others don't. The message is the same for everybody. We're brothers and sisters in Christ and I love them, all of them."

"A lot of us miss you," he said again.

I met Cassie on the doorstep and the news about the two million spilled out—"Praise the Lord," she said—followed by the news about the education bequest. She stared, then sprinted into the kitchen where the kids busied themselves at the table with after-school milk and cookies. She clasped each one in turn in a close, almost violently intense hug that lifted them from their seats. The kids hugged back instinctively, though bewildered.

"Mom?" said the oldest.

"Because we have an awesome God, because you are awesome children and because I had to do something physical."

They looked at each other, accepted it as sufficient explanation and returned to the snacks.

I told Cassie about the plaque then. She started giggling before I finished and we wound up in a mutual, coughing, back-slapping fit. The children joined in from the sheer contagion of it. When we finally calmed a bit, the question came, "Mom? Dad? Why are we laughing?"

Cassie answered.

"Because our friend Herb reached down from heaven to test your daddy one last time, just for the fun of it."

THE MARBLE KING

For the rest of the day and evening, we broke into laughter every time one of us caught the other's eye.

In the morning, while I fixed the window pane, the house quiet with the kids in school, Cassie came to me and the laughter got stuck somewhere and we were crying, smiling, too, that sort of crying.

David Bellin

David Bellin is a retired advertising executive, the winner of a CLIO statuette, the ad world's "Oscar." He and his wife live in the dairy farm and vineyard countryside of New York State's Finger Lakes.

An avid amateur historian, he set his first novel, *The Children's War*, amid the sectarian battles of Northern Ireland and the second, *Sherman's Chaplain*, during the United States Civil War. The San Francisco Review noted about that volume, "It encourages the reader to question the ethics of war and how it complicates our understanding of 'Do Unto Others.'"

"That's more than a wartime question, though," Bellin comments. "We don't leave our contradictions on the battlefield. I wanted to move from wartime to the inner conflicts we carry with us in ordinary settings and the moral choices we make every day. I think they're as dramatic as any clash of armies and they do change lives.

"But I believe we make a mistake if we try to handle our choices without absolute precepts to guide us. 'Do Unto Others,' with its ringing clarity, and the resonance of a higher power, is a prime example. I look for it in any fiction I read and try to make it the subtext of any fiction I write."

CPSIA information can be obtained at www.ICGtesting.com
Printed in the USA
BVOW07*1738230215

388128BV00002BA/2/P